VILI

FLEETING SNOW

PAVEL VILIKOVSKÝ

FLEETING
SnOW

Translated from the Slovak by
Julia and Peter Sherwood

istrosbooks

CONTENTS

Fleeting Snow by Pavel Vilikovský

The sections in this book are marked by numbers and letters of the alphabet. It is intended as a helpful gesture towards the reader, suggesting a number of musical motives that flow together towards a finale.

1.a Here's the thing: my name has lost its meaning for me. It has palled on me. Every time I empty my postbox and see my name on an envelope I think to myself: someone is writing to this person again! Why don't they leave him alone? And what's he to me anyway, why should I read his letters? Do the writers of these letters have any idea who they are addressing? Well, maybe they do, but I don't. All sorts of people can go by the same name, but I've got fed up with dancing to just any tune that might pop into someone's head.

I know what the person they have in mind looks like but I don't identify with him. If I caught sight of him in the street I would cross over to the other side.

1.b If, as the saying goes, every person is unique, their name ought to be unique too. Except that it doesn't work like that. What is unique about, say, Štefan Kováč, whose name is about as common as Stephen Smith is in English? In this country, no first name can ever be truly unique – the Church and the clerks at the register office have seen to that – and if your surname happens to be Kováč to boot, you've had it: you'll end up being known as Kováč Up the Valley, or Kováč the son of Lipták, or Kováč the Potter, as opposed to Kováč the Shepherd. Slovak is a garrulous language, we don't mind throwing in an extra word here and there, but even with that additional piece of information, does a name convey anything unique about a person? And even if we domesticate Štefan, what unique information do we glean from that? The familiar form 'Števo' conjures up the image of a blond, pink-cheeked softie, always willing to chop wood for the old lady next door, while someone known by another common form of the name, 'Pišta', would be a swarthy cunning prankster, maybe with a moustache, who will go far. Not to mention 'Kováč' who I will always imagine forging his own lucky horseshoe. There would be no point looking for anything unique in such images.

The purpose of a name is to help us pigeonhole a person. It makes life easier.

1.c If we ever came to truly understand someone, to know them completely as a unique person, a unique name for them might just occur to us of its own accord. But who would be prepared to make this kind of effort nowadays? It would be easier to give people numbers instead of names. There are official bodies that do exactly that, though for their particular reasons.

To be unique means to be beautiful in one's own way. Official bodies are not interested in beauty, all they want is to keep an accurate record of us. They don't see us as unique beings, only as numbers.

1.d My name is not Štefan Kováč. My name is Čimborazka. I am a self-declared Čimborazka.

2.a Here's the thing: whenever I look in the mirror while shaving, I recognise some feature of some distant relative in my face. A cousin, say. Or an uncle or, even more likely, my grandmother. Or perhaps I am my own step-twin – the same mother, two different fathers. Technically speaking it is just about conceivable, even though it wouldn't show our mother in the best possible light. But then again, amid the sheer unpredictability, the sheer randomness of life, what difference would a single, more or less unpredictable, random moment make? I, for one, wouldn't hold it against her. Such things do happen. You get engrossed in conversation, mental juices end up being exchanged, and so what are the bodies to do? They, too, become friendly, that's what bodies are like. Unless you are a clairvoyant, you can't predict what might happen in the course of a single day. And even if you could, you couldn't stop it happening.

Such things do happen. They have happened to me, too. It may have been – let's put it this way – a matter of social courtesy: you don't really want to talk to someone, so you make small talk instead. Or it may be just absent-mindedness, as if you were trying to solve an equation with three unknowns and suddenly bumped into an acquaintance in the street. Lost in thought, you say hello to him in passing but your acquaintance stops and you realise that a conversation is unavoidable. So you accommodate him, just to get it over with as quickly as possible so you can get back to your x's and y's.

Or, in a unique moment, someone might be revealed to you in their uniqueness. Things like that do happen. It happened to me, too, except that I didn't get pregnant in the process.

2.b Step-twins can look alike – they might be the spitting image of each other. Or they might turn out completely different, like night and day; it all depends on the physiological circumstances, a topic on which I am no expert. But then again, night and day also make up a single unit of 24 hours.

My twin both does and doesn't resemble me. When we look in the mirror we unquestionably share our basic features but it's as if life had moulded one of us with its right hand and the other with its left. When I see this face, I feel like a step-me. The sight sends a slight shiver down my spine, not because of our differences but because of our similarities. My eyes tell me that it takes so little, you just subtract a little here and add a little there, and lo and behold – a new version of the same model appears on the same chassis, with a different on-road performance. It is as if those skewed features in the mirror were the expression of a different, skewed character, and that's what terrifies me.

2.c A person's character is like the soul, no one has ever seen it. But that doesn't mean it doesn't exist. Anyone who wants one can have one. But I refuse. I resent being squeezed into a straitjacket, I want to stay fluid. I want to foam, churn and leak through the cracks.

I think what people mean by character is always behaving in the same way in the same situation; it's a formula that helps others work us out. And that's what I reject, I won't let any formula work me out. Take the homeless people who accost me in the street asking for small change so they can buy soup or a sandwich. Most of the time I ignore them and don't even felt guilty about it, but the other day in Heydukova Street, just as I was coming from the dentist's, a young man in a suit approached me saying he was short of money for his train fare to Trenčín. Other people before him had been short of money for a train fare and I felt no sympathy for them (after all, soup or a sandwich are more urgent needs) but he was the first to mention Trenčín specifically, and it was this that made me stop and listen to his story, of an unemployed man whose wife had thrown him out for being a layabout. He had come to Bratislava to look for a job and managed to find one, but it wasn't due to start for a couple of weeks, and he had now spent all his money, so he had to go back to Trenčín because you can claim unemployment benefit only in your permanent place of residence.

I don't know why it was he, of all people, who made me cave in. I didn't believe a word he said but I was impressed that he had gone to the trouble of making up a story; in his shoes, I doubt I would have had such presence of mind. As he talked, the man watched me bright-eyed and once he noticed that my defences were beginning to crumble he piled on more detail, coming up with a mother-in-law who was needling his wife about having to feed a layabout. Now on a roll, he was also, he continued, behind with his rent and he even outlined his prospective job in very concrete terms: he was joining the train-cleaning crew at the railway station. But I think it was the mention of Trenčín, right at the beginning, that did the trick, plus the fact that he kept smiling as he listed the various calamities that had befallen him. To cut a long story short, I gave him five euros and didn't even mind if he took me for a credulous fool.

2.d When I told this story to Štefan (I will use this official, neutral form of his name because neither Števo nor Pišta really suits him), he said: 'It's obvious what made you give in, you'd just been to the dentist's. You were relieved it was over and wanted to share your joy with someone.'

I didn't argue the point. I just wanted to show what a mistake it would be to draw far-reaching conclusions from my behaviour. To nail me to the cross of a character, metaphorically speaking. Can you tell if I am generous or kind from a single episode? And does the fact that for the rest of the year I haven't helped any other homeless unfortunate buy soup make me an insensitive scrooge? What about that bearded Rom I bumped into in front of the Dunaj department store only yesterday, on whom I bestowed a couple of coins to help him pay 25 euros for a room in the hostel where he lives with his small son (if you don't believe his story you can go and check it out for yourself; personally, I can't be bothered).

'I don't have a character', I said to Štefan, 'I refuse to have one. I have only moods, a different one every minute, that's all. I have not yet turned to stone. Accept me as being alive.'

Štefan said: 'I know why you refuse to admit to having a character. You're afraid it might be a formula based purely on the nature of your mistakes and failures.'

3.a Here's the thing: the avalanche has begun to roll. It can't yet be seen, it is still a long way off, but I can hear the first mass of snow pushing its way down the slope, rumbling quietly.

1.e I love native American place names like Mississauga, Petawawa, Maniwaki, Oshawa, Saginaw, Pukaskwa, Cheektowaga. These are English transcriptions of the original words but it makes no difference. To me they are unique; like brand names, they don't carry any other meaning, they mean only what they designate. My brand name is Čimborazka. It is the Slovak transcription of an original word that doesn't exist in any language.

Štefan would say that its English transcription might be something like *Cheemborazkah*, with the main stress on the first syllable and a secondary stress on the first element of '*razkah*'. It would make quite a nice native American place name, with its two bilabial consonants back to back.

Štefan's surname doesn't need an English transcription although the pronunciation would be different, 'Kovack', instead of how we say it, 'Kovach'. Though it would be even easier to just translate it as Smith. In English, too, it is one of the most frequent, most ordinary names. The one people use when they wish to remain anonymous.

4.a Here's the thing: Štefan is a scholar. He has recently had a book published by a university press somewhere in the northern part of the US. The book is called 'The Expressive Role of the Acoustic Correlates of Bilabial Consonants in the Language of the Menominee Nation of North America', or something like that. I forget the exact title, all I can remember are some of the place names.

Štefan is a successful scholar. After all, an American university press wouldn't publish just anyone. As far as I know, no one in Europe has studied the Menominee language, and in the US, too, there is just one professor at that university who does. He was the one to draw Štefan's scholarly attention to this topic when he spent six months on a fellowship in the US in the more politically relaxed 1960s.

The university sent Štefan the ten author's copies promised in the contract but instead of the parcel the postman brought him a summons to the customs office located at the back of Post Office No. 2–3 in Tomášikova Street. The officials wanted to charge him customs duty on the consignment. Štefan tried to explain that it was his author's copies but they wouldn't listen. One of the officials saw that on the envelope the price of a copy was given as $15.95 and he calculated the duty based on that figure, on the assumption that Štefan was going to sell the books. Only after Štefan gave him the Slovak translation of the title did he realise that a book on this subject, and written in English at that, would be impossible to sell in Slovakia. So he exempted him from paying the customs duty and Štefan headed for the bus stop with the cardboard box under his arm.

2.e 'By the way', Štefan said, 'now that you've brought up homeless people, I think that's a misleading term. They should really be called home-everywhere people. They have no permanent place of abode – their home is wherever they put their plastic bags.'

This was hard to disagree with, so I nodded.

'But you're quite a different kettle of fish', Štefan said. 'You pretend to be a homeless person in terms of your character but I have worked out why you refuse to be confined to a single one. You fancy yourself as having lots of characters but you are quite wrong. There are no homeless people in terms of character, only people who pass themselves off as such.'

So that was the second, deeper reason he came up with to explain why I refuse to have a character. I would never have thought I would prove such an inspiration to him.

4.b Štefan's book was well received in scholarly circles. Well, scholarly circles may be a bit of an exaggeration, there is just one circle, and a very small one at that, but that doesn't detract from the book's scholarly value. Either way, the book won't sell in Slovakia where there are no native North Americans; and even in America it sold only two copies. The buyers were students of Štefan's professor. As far as I know, neither of them has a Menominee background, and the professor doesn't either. (He didn't need to buy a copy since he was the one who had recommended the book for publication and edited it.) You may well ask what significance and impact Štefan's oeuvre might have on the Menominees' life and language which, as he informs me, is a member of the Algonquian family.

The Menominee tribe is on the verge of extinction and so is their language. Apparently, the only person still alive with full command of the language is a very old native American woman, who is actually deaf and dumb. Even if she went to the trouble of studying the role of bilabial consonants it wouldn't be much use to her as she can only communicate in writing.

It is always a great loss when a language becomes extinct; every language is unique. I am sure that if the story of my life were told in the Menominee language it would be a different life. I would like to hear this version of the story but there is nobody to tell it, and I wouldn't understand it anyway.

To be honest, it is highly unlikely that the Menominee would be interested in my life. They have other things to worry about. An avalanche started rolling towards them a long time ago and now only a single, lone arm is left sticking out of the snow. Petawawa, Maniwaki. Beautiful cries. Cries for help.

'Congratulations', I said to Štefan after browsing through his book. 'Hats off. You might as well stick it up your arse, though you won't be able to fit all ten copies in there anyway.'

3.b 'The avalanche has started rolling', I said to Štefan. 'Except we can't see it yet.'

'You're imagining things. What you hear is the grass growing.'

'Absolutely not', I said. 'I can hear the first mass of snow pushing its way through the snowdrifts.'

1.f First names work differently in native American languages. That's not something I learnt from Štefan's research but from books on the Wild West. Except that these days the West is no wilder than the East and nobody reads cheap Westerns anymore.

Native Americans have names like Sitting Bull, Cawing Raven, Morning Dawn or maybe Bungler Whose Arrow Missed a Hare – polysynthetic Indian languages such as Menominee don't need as many words as Slovak to express this, they just stick all the bits together to make one long word. These names are quite picturesque and probably also unique, at least within a single tribe, but there is a problem with them similar to that of character. They tie a person permanently to a single phenomenon, action, or event, depriving them of the chance to change and evolve. Language is an unforgiving manacle.

5.a Here's the thing: it all started when I found an old photograph at the bottom of a drawer while cleaning. It was taken on our first date – actually, it wasn't even a proper date, we weren't quite sure at that point that it was one. Someone, probably a fellow student, snapped us sitting on a bench, caught in the act and smiling at the camera in embarrassment.

I showed my wife the photo: 'Look!' I thought it would make her smile, like it made me, this time not in embarrassment but rather smiling indulgently at those two silly young things. She stared at the photo for a long time; she didn't know where her glasses were so she held it close up and scrutinized it as if scouring it for fingerprints. In vain, for the only prints on it were mine, and now also hers. Eventually she asked: 'Who is that with you, some girlfriend of yours?'

'Of course it is', I said. I thought she was making a joke; after all, she recognised me without any problem, or at least guessed who I was. But she wasn't joking, she was simply a stranger to herself. She put the photograph to one side and gave me a questioning look, as if about to say: 'That's the first I've heard about this.'

'Yes', I went on, 'a girlfriend. This one here', I said, poking her in the ribs with a finger. She picked up the photo again, looked at it for a while and shook her head in disbelief.

I just laughed it off at the time.

2.f Although nobody has ever seen the soul, we assume that it exists. At least everyone talks about it as if the term referred to something specific and indisputable, even if it cannot be seen. After all, how many of us have ever seen atoms with our own eyes? Atoms are just a hypothesis, like the soul, and yet scientists speak of them as a proven fact. It is one of the little tricks we humans play: whenever something is beyond us, we invent a name for it, at the very least, or borrow one from some ancient language, and we feel more secure straight away.

The soul can't be seen because it is hidden inside the body. Strangely enough, we can't see even our own soul, we just know it's in there somewhere. What's even more strange is that all of it fits into our body even though we sense that it's somehow much bigger. That it transcends the body in every way.

There are several theories of the relationship between the body and the soul. One claims that the soul is inserted into in the body as if into a case, and once the case is battered and worn out, the soul departs and moves on – where to is anyone's guess. Maybe that Someone who placed the soul in the body to start with takes it back again. According to this theory, the soul does not wear out simultaneously with the body and even if it does, it may be recycled in hell, or purgatory, or heaven, depending on the degree of wear and tear. Another theory presumes that it is the body that produces the soul and once the body ceases to be operational, the soul too is extinguished. The soul factory closes down.

One can only theorise about the soul's characteristics. Is each of us issued with the same soul to begin with and after that it's up to us how we treat it and how it evolves? Or is a baby born with a harelip or congenital brain damage supplied with a soul that is different from a healthy one? And what if the soul is given once and for all and never changes, regardless of circumstances?

Be that as it may, the soul is a useful concept, one that is easy to work with. Anyone can project anything they like onto it.

1.g The Menominee are becoming extinct both as native Americans and as human beings. In their capacity as native Americans they become extinct when they leave their reservations and join the ranks of other American or Canadian citizens. They get an education, learn a trade, start a business or get a job, becoming car mechanics, lawyers, doctors, actors or social workers. The legendary jazz musician Jack Teagarden, for example, was a native American, but if you didn't know you would never have guessed. Sometimes he would perform with Louis Armstrong, a black man playing with a native American, but of course everyone could tell that Armstrong was black.

Štefan told me about this successful property developer in the US who was also a native American. Štefan couldn't remember his full name and referred to him as Jeff. He read in the paper that the man had been charged with the murder of his second wife, with whom he had been embroiled in a lawsuit over their million-dollar fortune and custody of their two sons, although that is irrelevant in our context. Jeff was only half native American because his father was of Scottish extraction; this kind of mixing of blood also contributes to the extinction of native Americans in their capacity as native Americans. His parents had divorced because his mother had allegedly taken to drink and was said to have been predisposed to other native American vices, so Jeff, who had not got on well with his mother, went to live with his father, while his sisters stayed with their mother. For many years he had not acknowledged his native American heritage but he suddenly remembered it when the court was about to seize his assets, and he hid some expensive building equipment on his tribe's reservation. The native Americans from his mother's tribe welcomed him in their midst like a prodigal son and bestowed an Indian name on him – Withered Branch, say, or Stray Caribou – as well as some property he was entitled to as a member of the tribe. (Incidentally, Stray Caribou was not a Menominee, his mother had been a Shawnee.) But once the immediate danger passed, Jeff left the reservation and turned his back on his heritage, dying for the second time in his capacity as a native American. As a human being he might still be alive, but one day he will also die as a human being, like everyone else.

Native Americans who live on reservations could be said to be professional native Americans. This is not a demanding job, as they have received generous government subsidies in compensation for their lost territories and hunting grounds. Still, it is hard to be a native American if you can't behave like one. The life of present-day native Americans bears no resemblance to that of their ancestors. They no longer hunt animals for food or fur to keep out the cold; in fact there are no wild animals left on the reservations and even if there were, they would be scared off by the roar of the motorbikes as the natives race through the woods. When they feel hungry they buy their meat – deboned and pre-carved – in a supermarket or, what's even simpler, grab a hamburger in the nearest fast food joint. And as for fur coats or thick quilted jackets, they can choose anything they fancy from a department store. The women no longer harvest crops for nourishment, nor do they sew clothes from leather, except as souvenirs for tourists if they feel like it. It is a comfortable way of life but as time goes by many realise that something is missing. They might use a different term for this void. We call it meaning or purpose.

The purpose of life is to be lived. From a personal point of view this is quite a good purpose especially since, if you want to survive, you have little time left to ponder the purpose of life. But human beings seem to be designed in such a way that as soon as they have a free moment they start wondering about silly things, for example why they came into this world in the first place and what their mission in life is. Native Americans are no exception and as they have plenty of time on their hands and the questions keep haunting them, they keep them at bay with alcohol and drugs; as they are unable to find any answers, they prefer to forget the questions. They could seek advice from their council of elders, provided such a thing still exists on their reservation, but their elders grew up in very different circumstances and their advice would be of little use to the young. And so the native Americans living on reservations remain native Americans for the rest of their lives but they become extinct as human beings, with their health ruined and tormented to death by the void.

Admittedly, all I know about native Americans is what I picked up from trashy Westerns, set in an era when they had not yet been driven onto reservations, or from Štefan, who has never set foot in an Indian reservation. He hasn't even learned the Menominee language. There would be no point since there is no one he could chat with. He just learned individual words, primarily those containing bilabial consonants, but without understanding their meaning. He didn't need to learn the language. Based on his study of the phonetics of their language he concluded that the Menominee had once been a particularly fearless and ferocious tribe. But that was a long time ago, before the avalanche.

2.g The homeless man I met in Heydukova Street could have been living in some suburb of Bratislava, say Trnávka or Karlova Ves, and he may have picked Trenčín out of a hat, on spec, but it certainly was a fortunate choice. He did grab me, not sure if by the heartstrings or by the balls, I didn't have time to worry about that at first. What is it about Trenčín, as opposed to other Slovak towns such as Piešťany, Púchov or Považská Bystrica? Is it the fact that its name starts with a T rather than a P? I only worked that out later, after the homeless man and I went our separate ways.

There was an older memory of Trenčín lodged in my mind, somewhere deep down, almost completely buried under a layer of mud. I could hardly see it anymore. It went back a long way, to the time immediately after the war; I can't even remember exactly how old I was, maybe eight or nine. My mother and I had visited Trenčín. We were on a special mission. It had to do with a fur coat.

Before being swept away by the whirlwind of the war, a friend or an acquaintance of Mother's, who I no longer remember as I was too young at the time, had given her a fur coat for safe-keeping. For all I know, it might have been my father or the father of my step-twin, I never asked Mother about it. I don't know why this person was concerned about the fur coat, perhaps he was Jewish and Jews were prohibited from owning fur coats, or maybe he had an inkling that in those tempestuous times it would be hard to save not just a fur coat but even one's bare skin; in any case he didn't come back to claim it after the war. Unless memory fails me, he never came back at all. After a year or two Mother found that the coat was in the way, not so much in her wardrobe as in her soul, which is worse because, although a soul is larger than a body or a wardrobe, a wardrobe is far less troubled by the presence of someone else's fur coat. She knew that this friend had a brother living in Trenčín; she didn't know his address but discovered that the wife of this brother worked at the local hospital and decided she would hand over the coat to her. In hindsight, I guess it was a skeleton in the cupboard that she wanted to be rid at all costs, but all she said to me then was that what doesn't belong to us ought to be handed back.

There are two sides to memory, as to a coin. Heads, the lighter side, tends to leave a deeper mark in a child's memory. I hadn't travelled much by train before then. It was a sunny summer's day, the countryside rolling by in the opposite direction was all new to me, and despite the warnings of *Nicht hinauslehnen, Ne pas se pencher en dehors* and *È pericoloso sporgersi*, and despite Mother's admonitions I kept sticking my head out of the window until a spark from the engine flew into my eye. It didn't frighten me,

I would even say it just enhanced my sense that this was a unique experience, as did the salami sandwich Mother had prepared for the trip. Ever since then, salami sandwiches have been inextricably linked in my mind with journeys, except that now I buy them from a stall at the station and they are called baguettes.

So this was the light, cheerful side of the coin, which included the warm breeze in my hair and the blasts of steam splashing my face. The tails side of the coin was dark – I'm not saying it was menacing or sinister, just incomprehensible to a child's mind. I can't remember how we got to the hospital because I was spellbound by the sight of the castle towering above the town like a strict history teacher; all I remember is a consulting room with a bed or bench covered in white oilcloth and colourful pictures of organs of the human body on the walls, which were unlike anything I had ever seen before. I don't even recall what kind of surgery it was, what illnesses the doctor specialised in, only that, as soon as we appeared at the door, she pointed out to Mother that she didn't treat children. Mother said she was there about a private matter and proceeded to unpack the fur coat she had wrapped in brown paper and tied up with string.

At first I didn't pay attention to their conversation, gawping at the pictures instead. I assumed that the transfer of a fur coat between two grown-ups – the doctor was about Mother's age – would be a straightforward affair, a simple handover. But the string on the package got tangled up and they raised their voices. I can't recall their conversation word for word, but basically the doctor wasn't asking questions but protesting – what kind of fur coat was it, where did it come from, she knew nothing about any fur coat and what did it have to do with her. Mother, on the other hand – rather like the song whose lyrics go something like 'the one I love is not around so I might as well fall in love with the one who is' – insisted she had only taken the fur coat for safekeeping and now, since its owner hadn't come back to claim it, she wanted to return it to his brother as his next of kin and heir. After all, it was a good quality fur coat and he could surely use it in these difficult times.

Up until that point I had taken no interest in the fur coat. It was too big for me, and since nobody in our family had ever owned one, I had nothing to compare it with. The material on the outside was cloth and the lining on the inside was grey-ish-beige fur, rabbit or maybe dog. To me it was rather like a dog that had happened to stray into our house and moved on once it warmed up a little. I was happy that the fur coat had brought me to Trenčín and as far as I was concerned that was all there was to it. I couldn't understand how it could possibly give rise to an argument.

'How do you know', the doctor said, 'that he could use it? You can't have any idea.'

I was struck by how quiet her voice had suddenly become after the loud protests; I turned my head away from the pictures and pricked up my ears, which is why I remember her exact words. The word *definitely* in particular, as it sounded sarcastic to me. It is usually things we don't understand that we remember best.

'Oh yes, he'll *definitely* be happy about his brother's fur coat', the doctor said, 'seeing as he has no idea that he's got a brother. You can't imagine what it's like. He doesn't even know his own name anymore. He doesn't know if it's spring or summer, what month it is, or the day of the week. He might even get the year wrong.'

She paused between sentences, as if wondering if she could bring herself to utter the next one, and if her listener was worth it. Whether she should make the effort on her account.

'Yes, the fur coat might come in handy in winter, that's for sure', she said. 'It will be a bit too big for him now but never mind. I'm sure it could be taken in. But who cares about winter, he might not live to see the winter anyway.'

'I am really sorry, Mrs Königová', Mother said.

'It's Mrs Kráľová', the doctor corrected her. 'I still remember my own name. But your fur coat really is the last thing on my mind.'

'I'm sorry, I made a mistake, Mrs Kráľová. I am truly sorry about your husband, I just wanted to do the right thing. The fur coat isn't mine. I made this trip specially to return it and I can assure you that I'm not taking it back.'

Or words to that effect. Now, after all these years, the doctor's face has started to emerge from under the mud; it was an ordinary face, pretty in an uremarkable way except for two bitter lines around the mouth, the kind people develop when they have to give bad news regularly. Mother flung the fur coat, half-unwrapped as it was, onto the oilcloth, and made for the door without saying goodbye; I remember saying 'I kiss your hand' to the doctor. Yes, I said I kiss your hand, I was only eight or nine years old, later I was too embarrassed to use this old-fashioned greeting.

1.h When I was a student I took a summer job delivering the post; Mother had pulled some strings to get me to fill in over the holiday season. I liked the work. First thing in the morning at the central post office the mail would be sorted by postal district, and each of us would stuff our pile of letters, parcels and cheques into a holdall (the wheelie shopping bags of today were still a distant dream) and set out on our rounds. It was basically up to us how we organised our time and route.

I used to pre-sort my mail by street and house number so that I wouldn't need to spend too much time rooting about in the huge holdall. As I stashed the letters in the bag I would read the names on the envelopes and tried to imagine what their owners looked like; it was a kind of private game, an additional bonus of the job. I wasn't attracted by obvious, down-to-earth names such as Kováč or Medveďová, Mrs Bear, which left little room for the imagination. But it was fascinating to guess what someone called Libaj, Bikšudová, Svačko or Kabuliaková, names that had no obvious meaning, might look like. In those days, many old tenements still lacked letterboxes, and recorded letters, summonses and cheques had to be signed for. And so, in the course of six weeks, I got to meet most of the addressees. I forget what Bikšudová looked like but remember that I had imagined Svačko as a smiling, talkative old man with a twinkle in his eye; I even expected him to let me keep some small change from his pension with a generous wave of the hand. I pictured Libaj as a sturdy man with an upturned Hungarian moustache and a fob watch dangling from his waistcoat, and Kabuliaková as a frowning woman in an apron, with beads of sweat on her brow and smoothly combed grey hair parted in the middle.

On occasion my predictions turned out to be fairly accurate, though not absolutely spot on, but the reason I remember these three people is that they proved me totally wrong: Libaj was a young man with a crew-cut and dressed in vest and shorts; Kabuliaková had bright red fingernails and her perfume filled the entire hallway; and Svačko was a typical boring bureaucrat who reached straight for the pen without giving me a glance.

Not only are our names not unique but, unlike native American names, they don't tell us anything about their bearers. They are just lottery tickets that a parrot has pulled out of the drum.

The owner of the fur coat, Mr König, wasn't happy with the parrot's choice – one minute he was a German king, König, and the next a Slovak one, Kráľ. If I saw these names on an envelope, each one would conjure up a completely different image. But back then I couldn't imagine that a man might have no qualms about changing his name, yet be unable to recognise it later on.

My name wasn't picked by a parrot either, I chose it myself. My name is Čimborazka. Except I haven't told anyone.

2.h Afterwards Mother and I waited for the train in a park by the station. I expected Mother to be relieved to have the coat literally off her hands and that she would, now unburdened, perhaps take me for a walk around town, but she just sat next to me on the bench without a word, squinting in the sun. Eventually she said: 'Who does she think she is? Is she the only one in the world who's had to watch someone dear to her die?' But her question wasn't addressed to me. She didn't even glance at me, she knew I couldn't answer.

Honestly selfish as children are, they lay claim to their mother in her entirety, without allowing her an independent, separate purpose in life. A mother exists in order to be mother, that's what she is for. Only years later, when we are much older, do we realise that she is a complete person in her own right, like anyone else, like us, that she exists even when we can't see her and don't need her, and we learn to accept that. I had never understood the fur coat story but I hadn't given it much thought either; I thought we had gone on a day trip and this was just a small chore to be dealt with. Now that we had got it out of the way, I stopped thinking about it and couldn't understand what Mother was talking about. I didn't realise that this was the noise generated by the soul-producing factory.

It was a brilliant sunny day, with train engines whistling and puffing beyond the trees, and before we boarded our carriage, Mother bought me some ice cream from a street seller plying his trade from a tricycle. I didn't even notice that it had started to snow.

1.i The second of the Ten Commandments says: 'Thou shalt not take the name of the Lord thy God in vain.' To me this doesn't make any sense, for how can we take his name in vain if the Lord doesn't have one? A six-year-old Down's syndrome girl put her finger on it when she said: 'God makes the wind and God makes the rain but he has no surname.' Let me just add that, in fact, God doesn't have a Christian name either, 'God' is just a designation of his office.

Things were different in antiquity, in the time of the ancient Greeks and Romans; they had so many gods they had to give them names to tell them apart and they had allocated each their own portfolio to stop them from stepping on each other's toes. Native Americans in the Westerns call their god Manitou, even though Štefan claims that the Algonquian Indians, such as the Menominee, have no notion of God in our sense of the word and that they use the name Manitou to refer to the mysterious, impersonal magic force that rules all Nature.

We have only one God, albeit a tripartite one – the Trinity is jointly and inseparably composed of the Father, the Son and the Holy Spirit. However, these are not names, just terms denoting their familial relations. Jesus Christ, too, is just the Son's worldly, civilian name, one he used during his temporary stay among people on earth. We imagine the Holy Spirit as a carrier pigeon flying around the world and consecrating everything it alights on but it doesn't have a proper name either, just a title.

Our God doesn't need a name because he is the One and Only, the unique One; in fact, he might be the only truly unique… what? Creature? Being?

'Do you think we are beings?' I asked Štefan. 'Would you refer to yourself by this term?'

As a man of science, Štefan is not keen on vague debates that lack a solid factual foundation.

'Provided we use the term simply to refer to a living being', he said, 'why not? But if you have some unique individual features in mind, I wouldn't be so sure.'

'I know I'm not unique', I said, 'but I treat myself as if I were. I do it to boost my confidence. I have nothing against "creature", I'm sure that's the correct term, but I feel more dignified as a "being".'

'The only thing unique about people is that they are all much of a muchness', Štefan said. 'Otherwise no research or study, no human science would be possible. We would have to study each individual separately and any conclusions would apply only to this one person.'

Being a scientist, he has no choice but to see things this way. But I think he takes everything too literally.

'Entire fields of science would collapse', he said. 'Psychology. Psychiatry. Mind you, these are not exact sciences. But take medicine in general. Where would we be if everyone suffered from their own, unique illness? And what about pedagogy? It would be impossible to apply any general rules, there would be no unified curricula and teaching methods, every pupil would have to have their own teacher. And the list could go on and on, ad infinitum.'

He was clearly warming to the subject, getting quite fired up.

'If people were truly unique', he said, 'everyone would have their own unique language and we wouldn't be able to communicate at all.'

And that would be it for the language of the Menominee, I thought, including bilabial consonants. So there's the rub for him, even though he wouldn't say so out loud. But I didn't want to stir things up any more.

'So, if you insist on being so precise', I said, 'on being such a stickler for exact terms, please tell me how you would define God. Who would you say He was? A creature? A being? Or something else?'

That gave him food for thought. 'An entity', he said in the end.

That sounded good and scientific, although to me it didn't sound particularly precise either. But God is such a useful term exactly because everyone can imagine it to mean whatever they want it to.

5.b

I thought it was a good idea, albeit a slightly sentimental one; Štefan might have gone as far as to call it kitschy but I didn't tell him what I was planning to do.

I hadn't taken my wife out for a long time so I invited her for lunch. It was just an excuse. She had been eating very little lately, she had no appetite and also seemed to have lost interest in cooking. She used to be a good cook, inventive, never one to follow recipes blindly. But nowadays she would often ask when we ate: 'Something seems to be missing, don't you think?' On one occasion it was fried onions, on another it was marjoram; sometimes she simply forgot to put any salt in the soup.

The lunch was an excuse but I didn't tell her that. I wanted it to be a surprise. She seemed strangely disconcerted or confused by my invitation; she took ages deciding what to wear, until eventually I had to point out that this was not some big social event, just an ordinary lunch for two.

I took her to Café Krym; this was part of my plan. After lunch, as we emerged into the sunshine, I motioned with my head towards the little park opposite. 'How about we go and sit down for a while?'

Nowadays there is little that is romantic about Šafárikovo Square: buses to Petržalka keep pulling out of the bus stop with loud creaks and groans, trams jangle and grind their teeth on the bend in front of the university, and a continuous stream of cars flows past both sides of the park. But she raised no objections and crossed the road obediently.

'Do you know where we are?' I asked when we sat down. 'Do you recognise this bench?'

She looked down at the bench, at the slats sticking out from under her skirt, then at me. She shook her head with a shy, hesitant smile.

'Go on, have a guess', I said. Some homeless people were camped around a bench a little further down; a woman with long dirty hair huddled amid a heap of plastic bags and two men with cigarettes and a green plastic bottle hovered above her.

'I really don't know', she said. 'We're in the park in Šafárikovo Square, aren't we?'

'That's right', I replied. 'And we're sitting in the exact same place, on the same bench as in that photo I showed you the other day. Ring any bells?'

To be honest, I wasn't sure if the bench really was in the exact same place and not a few metres further away; it was unlikely that it was the same bench after all those years, but that didn't matter. It might have been a childish and sentimental idea to try and rekindle the past but it was quite understandable coming from someone who had more past than future – after all, who would be happy to settle for such impoverishment? I foolishly continued to badger her, and it wasn't until much later that I realised how futile my attempts were.

'What did you think when I sat down beside you out of the blue?' I asked. 'If I remember rightly, it was just before the exams and I pretended I wanted to borrow your lecture notes.'

Lines appeared on her brow; eventually she shook her head again, with the same embarrassed smile – the way a bride might smile when she carves the wedding cake and drops a piece on the table.

'Oh, that was a long time ago, you see', she said. 'Who knows what I thought then? I probably thought you wanted to borrow my notes.'

We both laughed, as if she had said something amusing. For a moment it almost seemed as if she were flirting with me in a girlish way, as in the old days. That she had agreed to play along.

'And, all in all', I asked, 'what did you think of me then? What did you think I was like?'

She gave another laugh and shrugged her shoulders. 'Well, I hardly knew you then', she said. 'There were so many boys in our year, they're all a blur now.'

'But you must have thought something, surely', I said.

'Hm…' She had to stop and think. 'Well, you weren't bad looking', she said, smiling at me, 'you still aren't, lots of girls fancied you, I supose. But I think the best looking one was this tall, dark-haired fellow, he was doing classics I think, I forget his name. I'm sure you remember him.'

She leaned back on the bench and stretched out her legs. 'The sun is really nice and warm today', she said, squinting.

1.j My real name is Čimborazka but I haven't told anyone. What would be the point? It would be the same as changing your phone number: your friends will remember your new number but they will still use it to ring the same person as before, the same idea of a person. But I don't want to receive letters addressed to Dear Mr Čimborazka, which would be like addressing a different person each time. Čimborazka is a clean, blank sheet; a reminder that I am a person – not an entity, just a being, albeit a human one. And that every human possibility is therefore still open to me each and every time. It is a silent, secret challenge to honour my name.

Štefan would like this name as it contains two bilabial consonants next to each other, nicely holding hands. If he took the trouble to research it, he might reach the scientific conclusion that my character is fearless and ferocious. Well, tough luck, I am not a native American of the Menominee tribe and I refuse to have a character. I'm just a man. I am Čimborazka.

2.i Like it or not, a mother leaves an indelible mark on her child. Even after she has gone she continues to be part of us – in my case, part of my shoulder. I'd had a birthmark there since I came into this world, it had just been sitting there quietly and without bothering me. The only person it bothered was Štefan, who called it a beauty spot. He is a linguist but that doesn't mean he can make assumptions about my birthmark – he is free to call his own whatever he likes. The dictionary doesn't distinguish between these two expressions, treating them as synonyms but for me a birthmark is linked to giving birth, birth certificate, birthday, practical, tangible things, whereas a beauty spot relates to something more abstract, idealized. Štefan and I got into an argument on this subject. Admittedly, I am just an amateur and he is an expert, though more in the field of bilabial consonants in the Menominee language than on the Slovaks' relationship to their birth.

The birthmark couldn't have cared less about our argument, it just did its own thing. All of a sudden it started to grow. It struck me as inappropriate at my age: after all, all of me – from head to toe – had stopped growing at the age of 18, so I assumed the birthmark would come to its senses. But it didn't, and soon it was jutting out of my shoulder like an aerial. One day, as I anxiously checked on its progress, it started to speak to me out of the blue. 'You think you're the only one in the world this has happened to, that nobody before you had a birthmark that started growing?'

That was quite a challenge. To make sure the birthmark didn't get out of control, I decided to do what other people before me had done. The surgeon to whose care I entrusted myself wasn't endowed with the delicate, ascetic fingers of a violinist nor was he possessed of an incisive gaze that would, by itself, have removed my worn-out organs like a scalpel. He had the looks of a plump and kindly circus bear that loves the smell of damp sawdust and the little treats that life doles out. My birthmark didn't frighten him at all and while I was undressing, perhaps partly to dispel my fear of the intervention, he drew me into a conversation about hobbies and pastimes such as football, Czech film comedies and music. He confessed that as a young man he had been a Pink Floyd fan, but that he also loved Ian Anderson.

Someone more clued up than I am might have guessed what was coming but I was genuinely taken by surprise. After the nurse had led me to the adjoining procedure room, made me lie down on the operating table and given me a Mesocain shot, strange sounds rang out from nextdoor and the doctor appeared on the threshold in his white coat holding a flute to his mouth. Before the injection took effect, he managed to play two easy pieces; I recognised the second, the folk song *Kamaráti moji, tu ma nenechajte, pod lipku zelenú, pod lipku zelenú, tam ma pochovajte*. The lyrics – Hey, my friends, don't leave me here, under the green linden tree, under the linden tree, that's where you will bury me – were tailor-made for an outpatients' surgery.

During the procedure the doctor explained that although he had no ear or talent for music, he had decided to enrich his life by learning to play an instrument for his own delight and that of his patients.

'Is this musical bandage included in my insurance cover?' I asked. 'Or do the patients have to contribute out of their own pocket?'

'Oh no, it's all free of charge. On the house.' And to prove his point, while the nurse bandaged the wound, he gave an encore, *El Condor Pasa*, a favourite of the native Americans in our market-place. They are not Menominees though, they come from Peru.

Soon I was out of the surgery, minus birthmark. Now I was truly an orphan.

5.c It took me a long time to realise what was going on. It annoyed me that at some point she developed a kind of verbal tic she had not needed before and took to starting each sentence with 'Hang on'. On top of that she would often repeat something I had said as if she were hard of hearing – for example, I would tell her that Štefan had had a book published in America and her response would be: 'Hang on, he had a book published in America?' What an unpleasant and irritating habit, I thought, where did she pick it up? It seemed to forcibly tighten the reins on a freewheeling conversation, make my thoughts wander off and, disconcerted, I would no longer feel like resuming the conversation.

'Hang on, so you won't be home for lunch?' 'That's right, I won't, but I've already told you that, haven't I?' What was there to think about? What was there to hang on to? It made no sense to me.

1.k As for God, another question that comes to mind is whether it's harder not to believe in one God or not to believe in many. In my view things were easier for polytheists like the ancient Greeks or Romans, since they had a choice – a Greek fisherman could afford not to give a damn about Hermes or Aphrodite, whose services he didn't need, but that didn't make him an infidel: he still believed in Zeus and Poseidon. Or did Gods only come bundled in a single package? And if you didn't believe in one, you believed in none? I don't suppose I'll ever know.

It would seem that it is easier not to believe in just one God – you are done with it in one fell swoop. But we are talking about a single omnipotent God, who is in charge of the entire Universe and every sphere of life, and woe betide us if we have made the mistake of opting to be infidels. It can have far-reaching consequences. However, as I look around, not many people seem too concerned about this particular threat. When we are asked to fill in the box 'religion' in a census, we are happy to put down whatever faith we have been baptised in. More conservative or emotionally unstable individuals may attend church from time to time to pay God a visit, only to be disappointed to find Him not at home. Whether it is a majestic ancient cathedral or a friendly modern prayer house that we enter, it's our job to bring God with us. Like the tailors' workshops where clothes are made up out of the material the customer brings. We are making a huge mistake if we fool ourselves that God is sitting in the vestry with a glass of communion wine patiently waiting until we deign to enter.

It is not so much that we no longer believe, it's just that we are too busy to believe. We are running out of time. We are so preoccupied with our bodies, with making sure they are comfortable, that we have no time left for the soul. It is quite natural, of course: the body is visible, it is constantly before our eyes, but has anyone ever managed to point a finger at the soul? We rely on the old adage: a sound mind (as the heathens called the soul) in a sound body; we scrupulously look after our body trusting that it will, somehow, sort out the mind. It never even occurs to us that it might be the other way around, and that a sound mind could beget a sound body. Science has yet to prove this.

'Just look at yourself, you had the birthmark surgically removed from your shoulder, didn't you?' Štefan said to me. 'But not from your soul.'

'But you must remember', I replied, 'that all my marks are birthmarks by definition. Whether they're on my body or my soul.'

2.j I can no longer remember when they stopped issuing platform tickets at Bratislava railway station. Platforms entrances used to be guarded by station staff and anyone wishing to go further had to show a platform ticket, even if they were just seeing someone off. The platform tickets were small bits of brown card just like normal train tickets, and they cost sixty hellers, in the old currency. You also had to buy one if you were meeting a train, and you had to show your ticket again as you went out. I have to confess I miss platform tickets. They were a great litmus test.

There are a thousand different definitions of love. It is usually understood to be a raging emotional storm, a period of intense enchantment that, according to specialists – endocrinologists or sexologists – lasts around nine months or, in the case of hormonally better endowed individuals, up to a year. It would be more accurate to speak of infatuation but people who are drunk on emotion are not sticklers for accuracy. For them it's love from the word go, and even though they are merely infatuated, they are convinced they have found love everlasting.

I think this view is too narrow, it cleaves too tightly to the body and the endocrine glands. Many years ago, I came up with my own, one thousand and first, and more universal, definition: love is when we consider someone unique. This kind of love need not be exclusively erotic, the body doesn't have to play first fiddle in it, but I have learned that even this kind of love has a limited shelf-life – if you are in daily contact with someone, how long can they manage to remain unique? I discovered that this is only a passing phase, just like being in love; like any external coat of paint, uniqueness, too, wears thin with time. Štefan, who doesn't believe in human uniqueness, goes as far as to claim that it's just self-delusion or subconscious calculation: we tell ourselves that if we see another person as unique it means somebody else might find us, too, unique. Ergo we are not unique, full stop. Štefan is convinced that this universal belief in uniqueness is actually proof that people aren't unique at all.

'I know I'm not unique', I said, 'but what if that is, actually, proof of my uniqueness?' But Štefan is a scientist and has no sense of humour. I was only teasing him anyway – I believe I am just as unique as everyone else.

Nowadays I stick to a more modest, less all-embracing definition. I wouldn't wish to impose it on anyone but I am in no doubt that it is valid: love is when someone is about to depart and you feel there is something you must tell them. You know that what you have to say is urgent and important, even though it may not seem so at first, but you can't for the life of you remember what it is, or you are under time pressure and can't decide which one of the infinite number of things you have never told this person you should choose to say now, at such very short notice. But you don't give up hope until the last minute, and so you end up seeing off this person who is leaving all the way to their train; you don't mind queuing at the ticket office and spending sixty hellers on a platform ticket.

Well, this used to be the straightforward test, the touchstone of love that is missing today. You would have parted with an acquaintance or a friend by shaking hands on the station concourse or, if she was a woman, you would give each other a peck on the cheek, and that would have been the end of it. You would have turned on your heels without watching them walk down the stairs with their suitcase. It wouldn't even have occurred to you to see them off as far as the platform, nor would they have expected you to. There might have been an affinity, a mutual attraction between you and this person, but neither of you would have called it love.

You might say that using a platform ticket as a litmus test of love belittles this sacred emotion. However, what matters is not the time spent queuing for the ticket or the sixty hellers; even if it cost a hundred crowns we wouldn't hesitate. The ticket is a symbolic expression of our desperate inability to speak out, and of the hope that we might still succeed even if time is running out and we know in advance that we will fail. It's this bittersweet ache that is love, as far as I'm concerned, but I wouldn't dream of imposing my view on anyone else. One reason why love is such a popular concept is that everyone is free to make it mean whatever they like.

3.c The avalanche may still be in its embryonic phase, as the scientist Štefan would say, but it has already started kicking. You have only to place your hand on the bump to feel it move. But then again, who would do that when nobody even believes that we are living in pregnant times? Štefan says that what I hear is grass growing. He may be right but that is exactly why he should believe me: that with my keen sense of hearing I can also detect the first sheet of ice breaking off with a dry crackle. It is only a tiny sheet of ice, no larger than a small window pane in an old wooden cottage. It hasn't started tumbling down yet, it is just skidding along on its backside.

A long time ago, when the Lord saw that the wickedness of man on earth was great, and that every thought in his heart was evil, the Lord repented that he had made man on earth and decided to bring a flood of waters upon the earth. However, Noah was perfect and found favour in the eyes of the Lord, who advised him to build an ark from gopher wood, even providing him with detailed instructions on how to go about it. And thus, thanks to Noah and his generations, mankind was given a second chance. Later on God rained down burning sulphur on Sodom and Gomorrah but he saved Lot and his family. That is what He is like. It isn't His fault that Lot's wife looked back; that's what people are like. But since I believe it wasn't the Lord who has brought this particular avalanche upon mankind, we cannot count on His justice and mercy. It's a matter of chance who will bear its full weight and who will receive only a light dusting. But if God has indeed created everything, it means He has also created chance.

There may have been one or more avalanches, at various times and in various parts of the world. 'Who knows, maybe avalanches have struck throughout the history of mankind – remember the Menominee', I said to Štefan, 'but I'm now talking about the current one, the one that's heading our way. This one has been triggered by the people themselves because, in their half-hearted faith, they have stopped taking God seriously. They are no longer taking Him into account. Some naughty skier has veered off-piste and onto an open slope, or some irreverent mountain climber has conquered peaks so high that it's not snow that makes them white but rather the feathers angels shed in autumn to grow thicker winter plumage. Maybe what is hurtling towards us is not an avalanche of snow but one of feathers', I said to Štefan, can't yet be detected by the eye or ear. Be that as it may, once it strikes, we will not accept it as God's punishment. Instead, the motion that it was a natural disaster will be democratically carried by the majority.'

1.1 A foolish thought, but sometimes I can't help wondering: what does an identity card identify? The body or the soul?

At first blush, the answer is obvious especially if we have our present-day IDs in mind. In the old days identity cards used to include information relating to the soul, if only indirectly and without acknowledging it: after all it is not the body but the soul that receives an education, and the fact that we are single, or married or divorced, says something about our state of mind. Not that the authorities in the old days recognised the soul, they just wanted to map out every single individual, right down to the colour of their eyes and hair, but that's beside the point; we are still trying to divine the soul from the little plastic cards we have today, which reduce us to a mere body: our name, photo, date and place of birth.

We have simply become accustomed to reading between the lines, the body's lines. It is a subconscious process outside our control: just as the body produces the soul, so the soul produces meanings. We can't let things be just as they are, we feel compelled to assign everything a meaning, a goal, a purpose. And, metaphorically speaking, the soul is the meaning of the body. Without the soul there is no point to the body. It would be just a factory running on empty, generating a lot of noise and polluting the air.

5.d I used to call her Duška or Lienka. Her given name, according to her identity card, was Magdaléna, which seemed to me rather awkward. In fact, it was two names in one, like a washing powder, or a shampoo combined with conditioner: Magda with its two plosives in the middle, almost like swearing or spitting, and Léna, a young woman in a grubby apron feeding chickens in the yard. At home, they called her Magduška, which I found too long, but I called her Duška only in private, when no one else was around. In public this name would have been too similar to the cloying, petty bourgeois form of address *dušinka*, 'my dearest soul', which I find repulsive and which didn't suit her in the least: she was a woman with her head firmly screwed on, atop a proud, dogged neck. Of course, Lienka doesn't evoke that either; it's a name that isn't unique in any way, I just thought it was harmless – neither physically too tacky nor emotionally cloying. I certainly didn't see her as ladybird, which is what *lienka* means, more like a beetle with seven uncompromising black spots on its back, ready to spread its little wings whenever it felt like it and fly away.

Nowadays I am at a loss what to call her. I have always thought her beautiful – in her entirety, as a single piece – even though that became less important as the years went by; after five or six years, she was just she. But at some point, not long ago, her face suddenly seemed to become more beautiful. The lines around her mouth and eyes vanished, the skin on her forehead and cheeks became tauter, had I not known her I would have thought she'd had a facelift. It happened gradually, not from one day to the next, and I also became aware of it only little by little – one day I felt that her smile lost its sarcastic edge and suddenly started to spill over like a puddle because there was nothing to hold it back; on another occasion I missed the contemplative furrows on her brow, but thought it was just a one-off rather than an ongoing process.

One day, as she was putting on her make-up in front of the mirror – she had never devoted as much time to this as other women, although she had never completely denied her feminine nature either – she asked me, out of the blue: 'Do you think that my nose has grown? That it's got bigger?' I didn't think so, but it was was true that it stuck out from her blank face more than before. That was the first time I realised she had changed and that this change was complete and permanent, as if she had vacated her face. What remained was the charming, empty countenance of a Hollywood starlet, eager to be offered a role.

And since we are used to reading between the lines of the body, in my mind I now connected previous deviations from her behaviour that had, until then, seemed unrelated and acci-dental, as if they had been dictated by the change in her face. I wouldn't claim to know whether in the course of our lives our souls are shaped by our deeds, or if the soul is something that is given and unalterable once and for all, but it was as if she had started to show me a different face. Its far side, so to speak. Like the nape of her neck. Or as if her entire soul had simply turned its back to me.

When it comes to the body it is obvious that the body serves the purpose of producing the soul. But what is the purpose served by the soul?

4.c

So Štefan thinks that a formula for working me out would be based solely on the sum total of my mistakes and fail-ures. Fair enough. There certainly have been some of those, quite a few in fact.

I'm not all that concerned about my mistakes – we know that to err is human. A mistake is just a flawed intellectual operation for which we can't be called to account – nobody likes to make a mistake or does it on purpose. In other words, it's not our fault if we are idiots.

Failures are a different matter. A failure, as I understand it, is playing foul in a relationship. When we choose the easiest way out of a mess, we are not being considerate to others; we don't know how to behave in their presence, we feel uneasy around them. But unlike with mistakes, we are conscious of our failures and we feel that the people we have failed will never treat us the same way again. They may have lent us some money and even though they are not asking for it back, and may even have forgotten about it, we are conscious of our debt and hold it against them – why should we still be indebted to them? By what right? Are they better than us in some way?

I don't mean to say that we can't look them in the eye; that we can manage. After all, to fail is human, and surely it is the one who has never failed who should cast the first stone? We squash a little turd with our boot and pretend it was never there, and eventually we believe the lie ourselves. But after a failure we can never be exactly the same as before, and when our failures reach a critical mass we become different beings. That, however, is a fact of such staggering magnitude that we can never bring ourselves to admit it.

I tried to explain this difference to Štefan. 'The human mind is the pole that helps the tightrope walker keep his balance', I said. 'And sometimes, when the tightrope walker yanks the pole too hard, he falls. That's a mistake. We can sympathise with the tightrope walker or think that it serves him right because he made a mistake, but what matters is that he is the only one who falls and no one else is hurt. Whereas with a failure…'

'What's the point of all this brooding? You're making a mountain out of a molehill', said Štefan, who dislikes contrived metaphors and similes. For him a mistake is primarily a useful aid, without which scientific inquiry would be unimaginable. Trial and error is a method that helps us inch our way to the truth, albeit a temporary one, one that will last only until proved wrong by subsequent experiments. Science can never stand still at the current state of knowledge, the human mind keeps raising fresh questions and looking for new answers. And so on and so forth.

'To use a hackneyed example', Štefan said, 'people once believed that the Earth was flat and rested on the back of a whale. The work it took to convince us that it is the Earth that revolves around the Sun and not the other way round! Nowadays we've got much further in understanding the universe but we haven't yet reached the final stage.'

'You mean', I asked, 'that even at this moment we are mistaken?'

'Exactly', he said. 'Certainly seen from the vantage point of future knowledge. In fact, from this perspective there isn't a single moment in the entire history of humankind when our thinking wasn't based on false assumptions. But there's no need to draw catastrophic conclusions, this is quite normal. We've survived and we're here, aren't we?'

We were definitely here, there was no doubt about that. I nodded but I wondered what the Menominee might have had to say about that.

5.e We had never been in the habit of declaring our love for each other, not even in the early days. That was quite sensible, as each of us would, in any case, have had a different idea of what the word meant. But sometimes I would plant a kiss behind her ear. She had a dimple there, in addition to a bone. When I kissed the dimple, it held the same significance for both of us. We both experienced the same thing. I kissed the dimple behind her ear. There was nothing that needed to be changed about the statement or the fact.

To come out with declarations of love after all those years would have been ridiculous and made us feel self-conscious. When we went for a walk we never held hands, and only occasionally would she put her arm in mine – for example, when crossing the road or going up an escalator. We were aware of each other without touching. We breathed the same air and found it equally fragrant or foul. That is what I thought. That is enough, I thought, we need nothing more.

As I have said before, we weren't in the habit of tossing words around, we had other ways. One afternoon I came home and found her sitting in the living room lost in thought, her arms dropped in her lap. As I peered through the doorway she raised her head, gave me a smile and said: 'I'm so glad you've come.'

At first I found these words touching, I didn't remember her ever having said anything like that to me before. I thought she must have felt like caressing me – just like that, out of the blue, for no reason whatsoever, and I liked that. But then I went into the kitchen to put the shopping in the fridge and as I replayed the scene in my head, to savour it like a favourite film sequence, something brought me up short: she had welcomed me as if I were a visitor who had just arrived, unexpected and unannounced. Why should she be so pleased by my arrival, wasn't it quite natural? Where else would I have gone? After all, this was my home and I had just popped out to get something for dinner, hadn't I? But by the time I put the shopping away the niggling thought had passed.

'I'm so glad you've come', she said, with a smile that was surprised and, it seemed to me, a little sad.

4.d Štefan is a given, he exists once and for all. I mean, he never questions his own existence. He isn't concerned with himself, there are lots of other, more interesting things in the world. The opinions he holds are also firm, rigid – for example, he doesn't recognise the term soul, regarding it as unscientific. After all, we have the term consciousness, which is more accurate because we all have an idea, at least a rough one, of what it means.

'Have you noticed that we say that someone has lost consciousness', he said, 'but have you ever heard of someone losing their soul?'

'Not really, although I have read more than once of a soulless body.' Maybe Štefan doesn't read fiction, only scholarly books, but that's beside the point. The problem is that the term consciousness has been usurped by scientists, who have turned it into a house, a maze. The ground floor is filled with the sprawling Ego, the lower ground floor has been requisitioned by the Subconscious, and the basement is haunted by the tongue-tied Id, while the Superego resides on the upper floor where various spectres, whose names I forget, haunt the corridors. To put it simply, scientists have smashed consciousness to smithereens and it is hard to know which fragment you are holding in your hand at any one time. The soul is the iron casing that holds all these fragments together, or a simple wooden cottage if you will, where the whole family has gathered companionably to enjoy the warmth of the tiled stove. The only trouble is, Štefan is not keen on metaphors.

'Don't forget that neither psychology nor psychiatry is an exact science', he said. 'In fact, as far as they're concerned you can't even use the word science. They're both just a kind of reading from coffee grounds, nothing but conjecture that can be neither weighed nor measured. Or have you ever come across a unit of mental life? The Menominee had shamans to look after this domain and I don't think their results were any worse. Come to think of it, they might have been even more successful.'

In Štefan's view one thing was clear: the Menominee treated both their shamans and lunatics with respect.

2.k Whenever I was changing the dressing on my wound or putting ointment on it, I remembered the surgeon and his flute. This grown man – an expert in his field, a family man and so on – found a private hobby that gave him pleasure and, even more admirably, he had no compunction about sharing this pleasure with his patients. He knew he was far from perfect but he was not afraid that he might make a fool of himself or that a musically better educated patient might turn up his nose at his whistling. He didn't give a damn. He loved the smell of sawdust and disinfectant, children, Czech comedies, music, and his patients. People like this are said to be kind-hearted but I would hate to stuff him into some sort of suit of armour. Let's just say his soul had runneth over, spilling out of his body.

As for myself, I am not kind-hearted, and not just because I refuse to have a character. If I had to use a term of this kind, I would say I am slack-hearted. My soul doesn't reach out towards other people, it is preoccupied with itself. I have found no pastime simply to please myself and I would be hard pressed to find one that would please others. Of course, I too am familiar with the plain, widely-known commandment that we are to love one another, and am happy to admit that I'm not aware of a better one. But as soon as I tell myself: Love thy neighbour as you love thyself, I'm screwed. I like my creature comforts but maybe that is precisely why I don't really like myself, let alone love myself. In short: my neighbours would be waiting for my love in vain – you can't squeeze blood from a stone.

If Peter, a self-employed fisherman, had ever brought his new friend Jesus home, before they even crossed the threshold Peter's mother would look at the dusty sandals on his feet and say to him: 'In this house we take off our shoes.' She might have offered her son's friend a drink of water but no coffee or biscuits, and after he had left, said to Peter: 'Don't you ever bring that unshaven tramp into my house again. Do you have any idea how he makes his living? He could be a mafioso or a drug dealer for all you know!' Between you and me, she wouldn't have been far out for, as we know, the bearded fellow was indeed peddling opium to the people.

I don't know how my mother might have reacted had I come home with a bearded, sandal-wearing friend. But one night a beggar woman – the word homeless person didn't exist in those days – installed herself in the corridor outside the door to our flat. As she tried to make herself comfortable on the cold tiles she was mumbling aloud to herself; Mother heard her and opened the door to see what was going on. After they exchanged a few words in the corridor, the beggar found herself in our hallway. She was an old woman with a crumpled face that looked as if scrunched up by someone's angry hand and darkened by exposure to harsh weather or maybe dirt, or perhaps she was a Gypsy – the term Roma was unknown in those days. She was the first beggar and maybe also the first Gypsy I had seen close up as she lay there on a rug in our hallway, in grubby clothes that may well have been lice-ridden. Mother laid a blanket for her on top of the rug and gave her another to cover herself with, made her a cup of tea – the woman didn't want anything else – and that was that. No, she didn't offer her a bed, we didn't really have that many rooms or beds to go around, but she didn't fight any mental battles with herself, nor did she ask herself the kinds of question about the woman I would find unavoidable today. Back then I was slightly scared of the beggar woman and also slightly repelled by her.

If a homeless woman were to put down her plastic bag on my doorstep today I wouldn't invite her in. Not because I would be scared of her or because she would repel me, although the latter can't be completely excluded. It's just that I don't let strangers into my house. Is it my fault that there are so many of us and that everyone is a stranger?

5.f In the early days, when I still called her Magda, I got to know the essence of the woman through her. She served as my learning aid, so to speak. Sure, I was in love, but more with the woman in her than with her in the woman. She may have been the only one, at the time, but she wasn't unique. I had no one to compare her with.

It never crossed my mind that it must have been the same for her. I was convinced she was attracted to my intelligence and the breadth of my knowledge, my wit, my bravura performance in seminars and maybe, to some extent, my Elvis quiff; sometimes I would show off boyishly in front of her by leaping over the metal railing in the park, or by opening a beer bottle with my teeth. In a word, I assumed she had succumbed to my charms. Many years later, when I asked her about this on the bench in Šafárikovo Square, I found that she no longer remembered. She was confusing me with other students, a tall dark-haired student of classics in particular, he was the one she had fancied most. I actually happen to remember that his name was Gutman. But he wasn't the person who had sat down next to her on this bench.

Never mind. Back in the old days I had leafed through her patiently, page by page – I can still recall how long it took me to reach the most exciting part of the female body. We weren't in a rush, working our way through our homework dutifully, starting with the textbook for beginners, moving on to the one for the intermediate students, and then gradually to that for the more advanced, until in due course, about a year later, we were ready to take the final exam. That was the first time I saw her completely, utterly naked. It happened in her house, when her parents had gone to visit some friends; they lived on the fourth floor and after less than an hour we started to prick up our ears every time we heard the humming of the lift to make sure we managed to throw our clothes back on in time. I must confess that I was far more nervous on this occasion than during my school leaving exam, which I had passed with flying colours.

How silly it seems after all these years! She played the woman's part for me although she didn't turn into a real, fully-fledged woman until a year or two into our marriage. It took her that long to find the courage to let herself off the leash. Mind you, who was I to judge, being an apprentice myself, but I am sure that I was partly to blame for the fact that it took her so long to reach maturity. I suppose I didn't generate enough heat. Thinking back on it now I would hazard the guess that, although a willing participant in this exploration, she had been driven more by curiosity than arousal. Maybe she resisted the arousal for fear that she might reveal some secret, one she may have been too shy to admit even to herself; I don't know and I no longer dare to ask her. She had never closed her eyes during our fumbling lovemaking, as if wanting to keep an eye on me and mirror my movements when necessary, and her breathing, too, was so light that it wouldn't have made a pigeon's feather fly away. Initially she was also self-conscious about being naked, or at least pretended to be so because she thought that was the right thing to do, but after she realised I liked her buttocks, she would turn to lie face down in a silent show of understanding, letting me admire them. And sometimes, when in a playful mood, she would even wiggle her rear to please me. Actually, you can't wiggle your rear when you're lying down; what she did was shake it from side to side or flex the muscles of her buttocks, I forget which. Sometimes she probably did the former, at other times the latter. A kind of little bonus, on the house.

Yes, she played the part of the woman for me and there were times when I longed to check if she was doing it right. You might think of these little episodes as failures, but I've never seen it that way. I don't approve of the fuss that people make about infidelity, this claiming of ownership rights over someone else's body and soul, as if they hadn't been given to us just temporarily, on loan. And anyway, I think the term infidelity as such is wrong, as these chance encounters had nothing to do with Lienka. She was the indisputable, unquestionable She, while the others were just some other, completely different They; by contrast, on the opposite side, I was always me, always the same person, which really, in a way, made me monogamous. I wasn't unfaithful to others, only faithful to myself.

I don't regard these escapades as failures – after all, God created serendipity so why resist it? In any case, each occasion served only to prove that Lienka acquitted herself well in the woman's part, in fact, maybe better than anyone else; and after years of practice in bed we gradually settled into a comfortable routine. She no longer looked over her shoulder wondering what I might think and followed her own route towards her own goal. We would look each other in the eye from time to time to check that the other was still there and having a good time. Our bodies did what bodies do, and that was it, without being troubled by any tensions or worries, and without our thoughts wandering.

The time it takes to work your way from the woman to the human being! And the effort! I failed, if I might put it that way, not in respect of the woman but in respect of the human being. I think these counted as my actual, genuine failures. The first, still unconscious failure, consisted in the fact that I got married without having any idea of what marriage entailed and that perhaps I wasn't cut out for it – although, let's face it, not many people can tell before tying the knot. My first real failure was that I didn't manage to secure a bigger flat for us, since I didn't realise how much she yearned to have a room of her own. I didn't think that it was particularly important. I didn't let her grow geraniums on the balcony because they would be in the way, I wouldn't do the rounds of doctors with her to find out which one of us was infertile and why, and when she suggested that we adopt a Down's syndrome baby, I went and bought her a dog instead. But my most fundamental and enduring failure consisted in the fact that my arms were longer than hers and I had kept her at arm's length, as if we were facing each other in a boxing ring and I was trying to prevent her from touching me in any sensitive area.

Was I worried that she would bite holes in me, like a mouse in cheese? You might say that we had different ways of measuring proximity and I showed no regard for hers. Come to think of it, she was actually, as people would say today, a victim of domestic violence. I never played the flute for her although I'm sure she would have loved a little music!

Early one evening, returning from a walk, she said, still in the doorway, with a frightened smile: 'Listen, you won't believe what's just happened to me. I got lost, right here in our street. I went into the block next door and only realised what had happened when I got to the second floor and saw the name on the door. I was so puzzled that for a moment I wasn't even sure where I was and what I was doing there. Can you believe that?'

I did believe her. Why shouldn't I? These things happen. It has indeed happened, though not yet to me.

'Soon you'll get lost in your own flat, you silly-billy', I joked. We both laughed.

3.d After us the deluge? Yes, that's how we behave but you need God to bring down the deluge. After us only an avalanche. I tell myself: oh well, at least there will be something left after us when we're gone. Sometimes I even sing to myself: *Hey, my dear friends, don't leave me here, under the white avalanche, under the white avalanche do bury me*. Except there's no point looking for gravediggers. An avalanche will bury us all by itself, personally, so to speak. It won't need anyone to give it a hand.

4.e Štefan acknowledges his mistakes with pride and why shouldn't he: he sees them as tourist signs pointing the way to the truth. If that was how I felt about my mistakes, I would freely acknowledge them, too.

For example, he likes recalling a snag he hit while studying bilabial consonants in the Menominee language: apparently the position of the consonants in certain words contradicted a working hypothesis he had developed earlier. Fortunately, this happened while he was still in the US and when he confided his problem to his colleague the professor, the latter offered to take him to meet a member of the tribe who lived in a small town nearby, I forget if it was called Tecumseh or Paw Paw. The man himself went by the name of Chuck Spender, his Indian name was Cross-Eyed Jackal, and he was a second-hand car dealer; he sold mainly motorbikes and go-karts but that's beside the point. When they asked him to pronounce some selected words – mostly local place names – they discovered that the English transcription was inaccurate, sometimes distorting the phonetics of the original, especially with regard to bilabial consonants. Štefan concluded that someone had simply lacked the requisite linguistic training, or just did a sloppy job, and this had resulted in a scientific error.

'Such cases are well-known in our part of the world as well', he said, 'mainly dating back to the Austro-Hungarian period.'

What he had in mind was that the priests who used to draw up birth certificates would often record names using the Hungarian spelling and word order because they didn't accept the Slovak one, or may have been unfamiliar with it. This was how Štefan's grandfather Tibor Kováč was turned into Kovács Tivadar. After the Great War, at the time of the first Czechoslovak Republic, he had his name Slovakized when he joined the civil service. He became a policeman.

'Nevertheless, for the rest of his life he went by Tibike, the Hungarian diminutive form of his name', Štefan chuckled.

I don't think he picked the best example because in this case the change was intentional rather than a mistake. However, it is not hard to guess why Štefan likes telling his American story: it proves that it wasn't his mistake but someone else's, and that provides him with an additional opportunity to flaunt his scientific intuition. He just shrugs off ordinary human mistakes that lead to a dead end instead of truth – such as people who see communism as the bright future of mankind, or Jack Teagarden as a white trombone player. As for failure, he will never consider it a category that might apply to him.

Štefan did have girlfriends, indeed quite a few, as he kept exchanging one for another before their warranty expired. He rarely spoke of them except for the odd remark. 'On Saturday I went to the University Ball with Jucka', he might say, but if I asked him a month later: 'So how's Jucka?' I would find that Jucka was yesterday's news and that he was now seeing a Žaneta. These were, at least on his part, relationships with limited liability and as far as I can tell, they didn't involve any emotional distress. Or at least he never admitted to any.

I'm not trying to say that he was secretive about his love affairs, rather that there was nothing to keep secret about them. He used his partners as a kind of air freshener, although I am sure he wouldn't approve of this metaphoric label; he merely claimed that, as a change from the sterile atmosphere of science, he felt the need to inhale some balmy feminine air. And once the fragrance from the air freshener evaporated he would obtain a new one; it was only logical. I don't know if you've noticed, but scientists attach great importance to logic.

If you don't place any demands on yourself you never fail in your own eyes. That, too, is logical and I am sure Štefan would agree, except I didn't say this to his face.

2.1 Actually, I also used to have a hobby. The technical term for it is graphology but we shouldn't let ourselves be fooled by the name. Štefan claims it's not a science and in this case, exceptionally, I agree with him. It is an art.

Many years ago, when I still worked as a teacher, one thing that struck me while marking students' exams was that every one of them had their own unique way of scribbling down their answers. I thought that was strange since at school they had all been taught to write by the same technique and using the same template. This may mean, I mused, that handwriting reflects what is unique about our soul, that this is where our soul breaks to the surface as we are gradually being moulded in the course of our own lives. For another thing that struck me was that handwriting doesn't emerge fully formed like Venus rising from the froth of the sea but rather it takes several years for its breasts to grow and hips to mature. It all started as a private little game: I would compare the facts I knew about a pupil with the distinctive features of his or her handwriting – for example, the notorious brawler Vančo would rip his words to shreds and cross his T's with an angry line, while the quiet, conscientious Holubec would draw his vowels like chubby piglets, adorning each with its own little tail, and I couldn't resist picturing him licking his lips as he did so. In this way, little by little, basically just for fun, I eventually developed a technique for interpreting people's handwriting as an expression of their mental traits, as I prefer to avoid using the word 'character'. I studied the footprints left by the invisible soul. Menominee Indians would have called me a tracker but knowing Štefan, he would have rather classified me as a shaman, or maybe even a lunatic. But he's not a native American and this activity wouldn't really gain his respect.

OK, I do admit that graphology is a pseudoscience like astrology, except that it divines from lines on paper instead of the stars. That doesn't bother me, being good at divining is an art regardless of what we divine from, and not everyone can do it. You need imagination. The problem was that I picked a hobby that wasn't going to make anyone happy – people don't like it when you rummage about inside them, and who would be happy to learn that they were divining material? But what is worse is that I have sold out, that I have monetized something that started as

54

a hobby, as unpaid art. I have been making a little money on the side as a handwriting expert for the courts, I am even officially accredited. By doing so I turned from an artist into a craftsman for hire, someone who isn't searching for the soul but instead trying to work out if a signature on a document is genuine or forged. This is something even an untrained police investigator can tell but I validate the finding with a stamp and my own signature. I can't even tell at this point if my own signature is genuine or forged, since my real name is now Čimborazka. Fortunately, I haven't told anyone yet so nobody is bothered.

But the worst thing of all is that since I have sold out I stopped deriving pleasure from my art. I can no longer track a soul with a pure mind just for the joy of discovery; it's as if I'm trying to find it merely in order to hand it over to the authorities. But I'm getting paid for it and, hey, you can't have everything.

1.m So Štefan's grandfather's name was Tibor, or Tivadar, according to his birth certificate. That was news to me. As was the fact that he had been known by the diminutive, Tibike. When I say this name out loud I picture a skinny, slender boy with a large head and protruding ears. He is blond, with a pudding bowl haircut and lively, keen eyes, quick at solving puzzles – if a Rubik cube landed in his lap, he would have solved it in thirty seconds flat. Štefan must have inherited those explorer genes from someone. But Tivadar and Tibike, these are names for two different persons, and if Štefan's grandfather had remained Tivadar his life would have taken quite a different turn. He would have become headmaster of the local grammar school, or a notary public in a provincial town, composed patriotic poetry in his spare time, or he would have dropped by the local casino for a game of cards in a dark suit with a bow tie.

Tibor, a.k.a. Tibike, was a policeman in the pre-war Czechoslovak Republic. But someone whom everyone knew as Tibike would have made a rather peculiar, homely law enforcement officer. He would most likely have dealt with cases of stolen chickens or domestic disputes by returning the goods to its owner, or with a friendly talking-to, and whenever he dropped by his local pub, the regulars would have bought him a drink straight away. But he didn't pass on to Štefan his affability and innate good nature, which was at odds with his official position, just as his name was at odds with his uniform. Nobody addresses Štefan by the Hungarian diminutive, Pistikám. He never goes to the pub and if at an international conference he happens to pop into the hotel bar with his fellow scholars, nobody buys him a drink. I think these people have different customs: they share only expert opinions and at bedtime everyone goes back to their hotel room drunk on their own, endlessly repeated, truths.

So much for Tibike. If you were to say the name Čimborazka out loud, it wouldn't conjure up any image because it would be the first time you would have come across such a name. And that's exactly what appeals to me: the name Čimborazka means everything to me but it means nothing to anyone else.

2.m Our flat feels sad now that it is so empty. It's not that I feel sad when I am there, I am used to being on my own and it doesn't make me feel lonely, in fact it suits me rather well. What I mean is that the flat is in mourning for her. The flat is missing her, as if it had been deprived of its soul. The two of them had something going that I had never been a part of and, to be honest, I was never really interested in. The flat won't have much fun with me and sometimes I can feel it glowering at me from the corners of every room. I suppose it remembers that I turned down Lienka's plea for new floral curtains in the living room – I saw nothing wrong with the old ones – or that I didn't approve her request for a new fitted wardrobe in the hallway. Thinking back now, why did I have a problem with that? It's not that a fitted wardrobe would have been in my way. It was just that I hated the idea of builders, of strangers hanging around the flat, I found it distressing. I am repelled by the insatiable human urge to be industrious, by the sedulousness we expend on improving and multiplying transient things as if they were to last forever. We make arrangements for permanent residency in this world and before we know it there won't be anywhere left without our imprint on it. Until – thank God, I tell myself as the thought crosses my mind – everything is buried under an avalanche.

Now the flat is missing her, it has lost its soul, and it is making me feel it but that doesn't bother me all that much. I don't mind if the flat and I are not on speaking terms, I really don't care. What bothers me more is imagining how much she must be missing the flat. I expect it must hurt like a phantom limb that has been amputated. It sheltered her little fiefdoms, her nooks and crannies, into which she could slip as into an embrace, but now she must feel exposed to the rough winds of that alien world out there. I picture her standing in the draught, looking around helplessly, not recognising anything. Not understanding anything. This thought depresses me and it must be obvious because one of the people who noticed was my old school friend Edo who, as it turned out, has lately reinvented himself as a yoga teacher.

'Depression', he said, diagnosing me there and then in the street and proposed treatment straight away. He said there were tried and tested ways of dealing with depression.

'Leave me alone with your yoga', I said, 'I'm too old for neck-breaking gymnastics.'

But what he had in mind wasn't yoga but philosophy. Had I ever heard of Zen Buddhism? Meditation? 'Surely you can manage to sit quietly and breathe, he said', patting me on the back. 'Come and see me at the gym on Thursday afternoon and we'll discuss it.'

When we were at school this same Edo had been a notorious wheeler-dealer, who trafficked in postage stamps, razor blade packets, matchboxes, cards with pictures of animals from the Hagenbeck zoo, and all kinds of other stuff we all collected in those days. Somehow, as if by magic, he managed to rip off his customers in every deal or transaction. He now sported a salt-and-pepper beard and long hair tied with a rubber band at the back, and in general was a dead ringer for St Constantine in one of those picture books for children aged nine and over. It transpired that he now called himself Ed because he had spent two years in America where he studied yoga and Zen with a Japanese master, known in Japan as 'sensei'.

The wheeler-dealer Edo and the Buddhist mystic Ed – drop a single letter and hey presto – what a personality change! I had no intention of going to see him at his gym and, to be honest, had forgotten all about him but yogis must have a sixth sense, because on Thursday morning he rang me to remind me of the promise which, as far as I recalled, I had never made. But since my flat and I had nothing to talk about and I had plenty of time on my hands, I thought I might as well spend some of it on a harmless distraction. It's not like I have any hobbies anyway.

5.g Things kept happening. In March, she got a cheque in the post, a refund on the annual electricity bill. She had always been the one in charge of everything to do with the flat, the two of them being close to each other, but on this occasion, she seemed to stare at the piece of paper in puzzlement, as if not comprehending what it was trying to tell her, perhaps a little scared of it.

'Why don't I come to the post office with you, just in case there are any problems? Don't forget to bring your ID, you remember the other day they wouldn't give you a registered letter without it.'

As a matter of principle, I had never applied my graphological skills to anything written by my friends or relatives. I thought it would be distasteful to pry into their souls in secret, behind their backs and, maybe, in a superstitious way, I was scared of what I might discover. There was something unseemly about that, I would tell myself. But of course, I was familiar with Lienka's handwriting, having been exposed to it on numerous occasions, and not even with the utmost determination can you be made to unsee something that you have already seen. Her handwriting was delicate, seemingly modest, yet defiantly leaning into the wind, with graceful arches culminating in sharp, pointed peaks. I had never allowed myself to draw any conclusions about her soul from this, selfishly allowing Lienka to retain a bit of her mystique, so let me just say that her handwriting was resolute, flung onto the paper like a javelin, with a flourish. The kind of handwriting that won't tolerate being talked back to.

While we waited our turn at the post office, she looked around nervously a couple of times, to make sure I was standing behind her. We got her ID ready in advance, she was holding it in her hand, and when I noticed her confusion I nodded in the direction of the clerk, to indicate that she should pass it over to her. The woman wrote down the ID number, counted out the money, pushed the cheque back to her and tapped on it with her finger: 'Sign here.'

This, it turned out, was the critical moment. She looked at me with frightened eyes: 'Hang on, am I supposed to sign here?' I nodded and passed her a biro on a string. She picked it up and moved it helplessly up and down in the air a few times but before I realised what was wrong I just pointed to the cheque and the dotted line for the signature. She gave a nod but kept fixing me with frightened, imploring eyes, until I worked it out and prompted her: 'Come on, write your name there! Magdaléna…'

And so it went on. She managed to sign her name eventually but every letter was unsteady, as if shivering with cold, and the signature wasn't like hers at all. I picked up the money from the counter, just to be on the safe side. The clerk gave us a long, suspicious stare as we walked away.

3.e 'Don't worry', I said to Štefan. 'People like you, who suffer from snow blindness, won't even notice that they're being buried under an avalanche. It will seem light to you, just a dusting, and if you lick it, it will taste sweet like candyfloss. You'll be wrong but who cares, humanity constantly gets things wrong, doesn't it? I mean, in terms of the future state of knowledge. You will survive but by the time you've acquired this knowledge it will be too late.'

Štefan gave a laugh. 'You're already up to your waist in the grass that you hear growing. Soon you'll be covered up to your head.'

4.f Even if Štefan had felt like dealing with nonsense of this kind, he had no time for avalanches since he was about to embark on a new project. Although he hadn't yet settled on a definitive title, the working version read: 'The Phonetic Expressiveness of Language as a Manifestion of Advanced National Linguistic Awareness and Character'. Initially he had also thought it might read '... an Expression of the Deep-Rootedness of a People in the Material World', but this type of research no longer seemed relevant in the new political climate and he assumed it would be more difficult to get a grant for it. Either way, terms such as 'advanced national linguistic awareness' or 'national character' didn't sound like exact science, as I told him straight away.

'Quite apart from the fact', I said, 'that you're announcing your conclusion before you've even started doing the research. Don't you think that isn't quite right? From a strictly scientific point of view?'

It turned out that I didn't know the first thing about scientific research. A proper researcher has to begin by defining the object and goal of their research, then proceed towards it by trial and error. Along the way the researcher adjusts their starting hypothesis as necessary and so it can happen that they reach an unexpected, sometimes contradictory result. But without setting themselves a goal and direction they don't know where they are going and get stuck.

Štefan freely admitted that terms such as 'national linguistic awareness' and 'national character' originate in sciences that are not exact, the ones known as the humanities. That was obvious. However, people who represent these fields also happen to sit on the grant committee and the whole point of coming up with a title is to win over the committee members. Once the grant has been approved he is the only one responsible for the research and nobody will put their oar in regardless of how often its title or goals may change.

'The fact is', I said, 'that you draw non-linguistic conclusions from linguistic phenomena. Do you regard this as scientifically sound? Aren't you worried that your linguistic research will expose your sociological or ethnographic roots?'

That was the least of his worries. Štefan believes that language is a fundamental means of communication, one that affects every sphere of life and thus cannot be pigeonholed. Or something to that effect, it would take up too much space to repeat his actual words.

'There's another rub', I said. 'It's that the Slovaks are not native Americans. They are a small, obscure nation and it's highly unlikely that anyone in America would ever publish a study of their advanced linguistic awareness. If I were you, I wouldn't count on it.'

But Štefan wouldn't be thrown off balance. 'At least there will be no need to traipse around customs offices', he said.

2.n 'I don't understand why I should be concerned about sitting in particular', I said to Edo. 'I'm constantly meditating about something, whether I'm standing, walking or sitting.'

'What you're talking about is not meditation', he said, 'it's musing, and that's a completely different kettle of fish. The exact opposite, in fact.'

I realised I had judged him too harshly. Not that he hadn't cheated with the Hagenbeck pictures and marbles, but nowadays, when it came to yoga, Zen and me, his intentions seemed to be honest. And also selfless – he wouldn't take a cent for the hour he spent with me in his small office next to the gym. He also freely shared the information that before heading for America, he had been a master of martial arts – karate, judo, taekwondo or kung fu, or whatever these things are called. In one of these disciplines he acquired a brown, or maybe even black, belt, I forget which, and it doesn't really matter anyway because he had since moved on to yoga as a higher, spiritual form of exercise.

'Yoga and Zen have changed my life radically', he declared, launching into an explanation of the three stages of Hatha Yoga but I stopped him in time and said I wasn't interested in physical exercise. 'All I want is to gain control of my mental state', I said, 'if such a thing is at all possible.' That was how we got to the subject of sitting. He demonstrated the correct cross-legged lotus position – I couldn't help but admire the flexibility and suppleness of his apparently burly and stocky body. He didn't even get out of breath as he explained that I had to keep my spine firm and upright, relax my shoulders aligning them with my ears, and align the crown of my head with the ceiling. I should draw in my chin because if I let it jut upwards my posture would slacken. I wasn't supposed to lean to the side, forwards or backwards but had to sit bolt upright, as if supporting the sky with my head. And that was just for starters. Once I succeeded in holding this posture I would also have achieved the right state of mind and wouldn't have to worry about anything else. There were quite a few do's and don'ts to begin with but then again, I had plenty of time, I told myself, and at least this was something that kept me occupied.

Two weeks later I received a call from the caring Ed. 'How is it going?' he asked.

'I'm working on it', I said. 'I'm having trouble crossing my legs, my stomach gets in the way and I keep getting cramp in my calves. Maybe it would also work without having to cross my legs?'

It turned out that it wouldn't, because it is precisely this leg position that overcomes the dualistic nature of the mind. This is based on the premiss that we have two legs, this one and the other, each of them separate, but by intertwining them in this way we turn them into a single leg, so to speak.

'We still have both our legs, you see, but at the same time we have only one. This symbolises the unifying of the world into a single whole, with all its contradictions.'

'That reminds me of something', I said, and recited a line by a revolutionary poet from our school textbook. 'There's only one world and yet there are two worlds', I said, but this didn't make Ed laugh – Edo was bottom of the class at school and I bet he had never learnt a poem by heart.

'Precisely', he replied. 'But you could also put it the other way around and say that there are two worlds, yet there is only one. Not everyone gets this straight away, so sometimes I use this example: if you think that your life ends in death, you are wrong. But you'd be just as wrong to assume that you aren't going to die. We all die and don't die at the same time, that's the right way of looking at it. Do you see what I'm driving at?'

'I certainly do', I replied. 'Whatever, as young people say nowadays.'

'Hm, I guess so', Ed agreed after some hesitation – maybe he just didn't care for the vernacular. 'The point is: it's all about keeping an open mind, a mind that is empty and receptive to everything.'

'That shouldn't be a problem', I said. 'Remember Babušková saying back in fifth grade that I had a hollow, empty head? The only thing that worries me is the crossing of the legs. I still have two and however hard I try, I can't turn them into one.'

5.h Here's the thing: I didn't believe her. Another failure on my part, you might say. I thought she was just pretending, that she was intentionally keeping me at arm's length. That she was punishing me by becoming distant. Not that I held it against her, from her point of view she had every right to do so. It's just that I was stupid.

Lienka had worked in an institution for disabled children for many years, first out of necessity, because she couldn't find any other job, but later she took an evening course in teaching children with special needs and judging by how much she talked about them at home and by what she said, she had developed strange, almost passionate feelings towards these unfortunate creatures. She would bring them *Tatranka* or *Marína* biscuits, which resulted in us having words. It was not a question of money, the biscuits weren't expensive, but I had asked if she used these treats as a reward in training, like you do with dogs, and that was a big mistake. Outraged by this comparison she berated me for talking about her children as if they had no soul. Her children! Around that time, on a couple of occasions, she brought one of them – Katinka, whom I used to call, jokingly, Miss D. – home for the weekend, presumably to break down my resistance to adoption but I just rebuked her for bringing her work home. Shortly after that, I got us Kora, a dachshund mongrel and from then on I was able to counter Lienka's argument by asking how she could be sure that dogs didn't have a soul. To be honest, I don't really know if they have one like we do, but

I had no doubt that Kora had an inner life – she could be happy or sad, she could take offence and, unlike people of Štefan's ilk, she had a sense of humour. The fun we used to have! For example, when we went out and I threw her a ball, she would fetch it five times obediently, but the sixth time she would drop it somewhere in the grass and keep barking loudly, demanding that I throw it again and would stick her tongue out at me with a mischievous grin. Either way, this question silenced Lienka because she could never deny that any living creature had a soul, maybe not even an ant.

So at first I didn't believe her as I assumed she was just pretending to be confused and baffled, that she was only feigning all these mistakes and missteps, that it was just something she had picked up from her charges, having observed them all those years. Actually, I did hold it against her – not the fact that she kept me at arm's length, which she was entitled to do given my behaviour in the marital arena – but that she had chosen such a crafty, sly way of getting back at me.

I first began to have doubts that this was just a game when I tried to snuggle up to her one night. We made love less frequently at our time of life, sometimes once every two or even four weeks, but each time she would meet me willingly at least halfway. On this occasion, though, when I began to kiss her, I felt her body stiffen under mine. No, she didn't try to put it down to tiredness or not being in the mood, she didn't resist with a single word or movement, but when I looked her in the face with an unspoken question, I was met by a confused, apprehensive gaze. At first I didn't let that stop me and rolled her nightdress up to her breasts – this signal had usually sufficed for her to take it off by herself – feeling my way all around her body to warm her up. But also to warm myself up, except that there was something puzzling about all this – the blanket that lay there pale and motionless like a stillborn child, or the silence that was too loud. I looked up and saw that she had raised her head slightly from the pillow and followed my hand in surprise, as if curious to see what I was looking for and if I would find it. All in a silent, uncomprehending way, as if she had no idea what was going on, as if this was the first time this had happened to her, and she had no clue how to deal with it. The thought flashed through my head that this wasn't something she could have picked up from her charges, she would have had no opportunity to do so, and after that I could no longer continue defiling a child. It felt as if I were snatching her body out of her hands by force and she couldn't defend herself against the theft. If it had been someone else maybe I wouldn't have cared, it might even have stoked my fire, but I had been used to receiving gifts from her. Suddenly I felt very lonely in the marital bed.

For the last time I kissed that delicate spot on her neck where you cut the throat, and we have never made love since. I couldn't get that sight out of my mind.

1.n I may have sold out, but perhaps I can still put my hobby to good use in a way that is intellectually enriching. The other day, as I was preparing an expert opinion on an obviously forged signature – the case involved suspected fraud in the purchase of a house – it occurred to me that I might be able to divine a person's real soul from the way they forge someone else's signature. Does the forger dive into the signature head first or does he first gingerly test the temperature of the water with his toes, carefully imitating every loop and curve? The act, or rather the offence, is the same and so is the penalty, and yet: what a difference! It is far greater than the basic difference between a risk taker and a cautious person, or between someone who is reckless and a pedant. The matter involves more subtle, and yet more telling, nuances, for example, how easy or difficult it is for a soul to resolve to take on a different guise and impersonate somebody else's name. In this particular case the suspect's name was Ďuriačik and he was quite reluctant to crawl into Baumgartner even though they came from the same town, so he wouldn't have needed to travel very far. He just about managed the two bulges on the *B* and the letter *a*, but he got entangled in the transition from *u* to *m* and by the time he reached *gartner* he had lost his nerve and his shaky undulations lacked the flair of the original. Whereas you could say that the latter climaxed joyfully in a flamboyant stroke of the pen, the Slovak guy was trying to sneak away from the alien, German environment without being noticed.

The court documents included a notarised certificate of purchase although in this particular case the signature was beyond any doubt. While the signature was clearly genuine, it was the certificate itself issued by the notary, Mr Bánovský, that was a forgery. As for Ďuriačik, maybe the reason he felt so ill at ease in Baumgartner's skin was that he bore a grudge against the Germans or maybe, although he was only used as a front-man in this affair, masquerading in this guise he may have felt like the back end of a pantomime horse.

No one writes by hand anymore and all official documents share the computer printer's soul, which leaves only signatures to divine from. Although, on a sunnier day, I might have enjoyed extracting Ďuriačik's real soul from the fake Baumgartner, at this moment it seemed a more pressing task to work on my own soul, but in addition to my uncooperative legs, I was hampered in this by problems with my breathing. Ed talked about three kinds of breathing: pectoral, abdominal and clavicular – I didn't have a clue what the last one was, and would have found it too embarrassing, as an A student, to grill a former classmate who had been bottom of the class.

4.g *Garazda. Furajtovať. Durgnúť. Gruľovník. Krčadlá.*
Homoždiť sa. Korčiašok. Chrúšťava.

'Nice words', I said to Štefan, 'they sound really evocative. I've never heard some of these before.'

'I'm sure you haven't, gems like these don't just lie about on the pavement for you to trip over, and you would look for them in vain in a superstore. Our Irenka here', he said, gesturing towards his PhD student, a black-feathered crow with dark eyes flitting from branch to branch, 'has travelled the length and breadth of Slovakia digging them up. She has ferreted them out, you might say, at the last minute, before they were overgrown by grass forever.'

With a proud, proprietary look, he studied the young woman as if she were his own invention. A particularly successful one.

'I bet you don't know what some of these words mean. For example, what do you think the meaning of *futrangoš* is?' he asked, his gaze still glued to his assistant.

I shook my head.

'Come on, Irenka, enlighten this ignoramus', he prompted the young woman.

'It means flibbertigibbet', she said with a shy, apologetic smile. As if uncomfortable, almost scared, to be cast in the role of a teacher, she made to leave – 'I must be off' – and was gone.

'Ah, Irenka, I see', I said when she closed the door. 'A new discovery? A nice rear end.'

Štefan didn't deem my question worthy of an answer. 'You can't take her rear out of context', was all he said.

'I'm sure she has plenty of assets', I said, 'it's just that I haven't yet had an opportunity to get acquainted with them. But I couldn't fail to notice her rear assets, they would have been impossible to ignore in those clinging trousers.'

But since Štefan lacks a sense of humour and didn't laugh, my punishment was to accuse him of exploiting a promising scholar by assigning her inferior menial tasks, and probably in all sorts of other ways as well – I said with a wink – since a girl in her position is frightened to say no. He denied it indignantly.

'This is a mutually beneficial collaboration', he said. 'I am no longer cut out for field work, I'm too old, while she can learn scientific procedures and methods by working with me. There's nothing more to it.'

'No need to keep secrets from me', I said. 'I'm your twin, after all, and monozygotic to boot.'

'Only my step-twin, don't you forget that', he replied unsmilingly. 'As for the single egg, that's nothing to boast about, nowadays you can even find five-egg pasta.'

From then on, we limited our discussions in his office at the institute to words. Štefan was at the stage when you can wallow endlessly in your project as it has yet to acquire a firm shape, and something that is still so nebulous is in no state to run into obstacles. He certainly wouldn't consider a layman like me an obstacle; I think he just wanted to admire his own reflection in the mirror of my astonishment.

'Listen to this one', he said. '*Čmrlákať sa*. What do you think this word means?'

He repeated it again, slowly, rolling it around his mouth, as one would when tasting a first, tentative sip of wine. '*Čmr – lá – kať. Sa*. Well?'

'I guess it's some kind of activity that's not entirely savoury', I said, 'but I have no idea what kind exactly.'

'It's a synonym of *babrať sa*. To dabble. Haven't heard it before, have you? But do you feel how much more apt *čmrlákať sa* is? The *čmr* screams disgust or contempt, and the long *lá* expresses the temporal component, suggesting that it's taking a long time and the speaker is losing his patience. All this neatly packaged into a single word.'

To regain his balance after my teasing Štefan needed to score a few more points like this. So I learned that *holazeň* is a forest clearing, *cobŕňať* means to spill, *kýšeľ* is a type of acidity, *gruňos* is a yokel, *galbáč* is a left-handed person and *holožvaj* means lazybones. Nor had I known that *gavurovať* means to talk back, *komprdovať* means to mollycoddle, and *kopirdan* is a bastard child, but I had to admit that these were lovely, juicy expressions. You could almost hear Štefan smacking his lips as he pronounced these words.

'You have to admire the commitment with which people used to approach life. The creative energy and – I'm not afraid to use this word – brilliant linguistic awareness with which they used to throw themselves into it, how they exploited the whole range of human sounds to express their feelings adequately. You mustn't forget that we're not talking about intellectuals here, these were people who may have been illiterate, but believe me, they knew how to deal with the world around them. We can only envy them their passion, their love of life.'

'Spot on', I said. 'For where have all these picturesque expressions gone? Here they are, lying on a table dissected by some academic who had previously studied bilabial consonants in the language of the native American tribe of the Menominees. Do you see the parallel?'

But Štefan was on a roll and just ignored my words.

'Listen to this one: *bľosa. Bľo – sa!*' he exclaimed. 'Do you know what it means? I'll be damned if you do, my friend! It's the blaze on the head of a horse or a cow.'

That was when I let my defences drop and allowed myself to be provoked.

'Let me give you a word for a change', I said, 'one that you have probably never come across. Čimborazka. Ring any bells?'

'How was that again? *Čimborazka?*' Štefan stopped to think for a moment. '*Čim – bo – raz – ka* ... sounds like a dialect word, wait a minute, let me guess. I think it might be a wooden bolt on a barn door. Or a special kind of scythe – for the grass that you can hear grow. Or it could be a nickname for the pub clown. You know, a regular who starts cracking jokes when he gets drunk. Although that should really be Čimborazko or Čimborázik.'

That was a cutting remark but when he saw that I shook my head he gave up and asked a direct question: 'OK, will you tell me what it means?'

'It means nothing', I said. 'It's a word that denotes what is left of a person after they've been pulled out from under an avalanche. The body may still be alive but it no longer produces a soul.'

'Bah', said Štefan. 'I knew it couldn't be a Slovak word, unless it came from some Góral village on the Polish border.'

After pondering this for a while the expert in him declared: 'In linguistic terms, it could also come from the village of Telgárt or Liptovská Teplička, although, as far as I know, they have never been struck by an avalanche. I wonder if it might come from that village under the Krížna Mountain, the one that got snowed in sometime between the two wars.'

'It originates in the Menominee language', I said, 'just like Petawawa or Maniwaki. Except that I don't remember the English transcription.'

But Štefan doesn't get jokes and he started giving me the spelling straight away.

2.0 My mother didn't hesitate to push me out into this world, she just plonked me onto my feet: off you go! She wasn't afraid of taking on this challenge even though the times and circumstances were hardly auspicious. However, Lienka and I were both afraid in our student days, she of her parents and I of premature responsibility. I guess that's what it was. I didn't think of it as a failure at the time, as it was our joint decision; rather, I told myself that the failure was that it happened in the first place, but we both had our fingers in that pie. As a matter of fact, my finger was the longer one and thus I bore the greater share of the guilt, while her only sin was her naïve trust in me. That is why, years later, I refused to do the rounds of the doctors with her, to make sure nobody would find out and say out loud that the problem wasn't in me and that Lienka was suffering the consequences of that past intervention. In a way, I was being considerate rather than a failure. Or had I, in fact, been afraid that she might feel I was responsible and secretly blame me?

These were the sorts of things going through my head for an hour as I sat on a rug in the living room crossed-legged, though not in a yoga position, only like a Turk. I was also thinking – once I managed to forget that my bum was getting sore and my erect spine was going numb – of those onomatopoeias of Štefan's that ooze emotions like juice from a ripe peach. *Bľosa!* A beautiful word, no doubt, but is there anyone these days who personally owns a cow with a white mark on the forehead, caressed ever so gently by this word? Nowadays factory-farmed cows provide the raw material for meat and milk, they don't have individual names and have to manage with a tattooed number or a tag in their ear. Even if a cowherd or a milkmaid developed an attachment to one of the animals in their care they would be too embarrassed to show it, and very soon there would be no cows left in this country anyway because this same raw material can be produced more cheaply elsewhere. Cows in this country are unprofitable, just like horses, and the word *bľosa* will go the way of domestic livestock because beauty, too, is unprofitable. The way of the avalanche, I'd say, although rigorous scientists aren't interested in this aspect of exact phenomena. It's outside their field of research.

Another word I liked was *kýšeľ*, which suggests a kind of acidity that had evolved naturally, without outside intervention, whereas the ostentatious artificiality of *kyslosť* or *kyslota*, the standard words for sourness and acidity, imply that they have come about as the result of a controlled chemical process. It also occurred to me that *hoľazeň* would be a perfect name for the emptiness of mind that Ed said I should strive for. However, if you have to think about *hoľazeň*, it means that you are miles away from it – that much I understood about Zen.

'This quiet hour has rather grown on me', I said to Ed when he grabbed me by the scruff of the neck over the phone, 'I start looking forward to it the moment I wake up in the morning. I'm just worried that I'm doing something wrong because all sorts of thoughts keep whirling round my head. I guess you would call my attempts musings rather than meditation.'

I chose not to admit that I cheated about crossing my legs because I had no intention of becoming a cripple for the sake of a spiritual exercise.

'OK, let's take this point by point', Ed said. 'First off, you shouldn't approach meditation with any feelings whatsoever, that is, you're not meant to look forward to it or worry about it. But these are common beginners' mistakes, don't let them put you off. It doesn't matter whether you do the exercise right or not, if you hit an obstacle, it's just a warning sign that you have the wrong attitude to the whole thing. There is no specific goal you're meant to achieve – I mean something that might tell you 'this is not the right way to exercise'. Even bad exercises are good provided you do them mindfully and keep doing them.'

And so on. My problems seemed to have made Ed happy and he carried on with his lecture for at least twenty minutes. One of the things I learned was that if it matters to me what I do, that, too, was a sign of dualism. When I eat, I eat and when I exercise, I should just exercise, and that's it. If I don't care about something, I'm unlikely to talk about it.

'But you're the one who rang me to ask how it's going', I said.

'All right, that's a different matter, a beginner can seek the advice of his teacher. His master or sensei, as the Zen Buddhists say.'

'The thing you have to remember', said my sensei, 'is that to study Buddhism means to study oneself. And studying oneself means forgetting oneself. That's the basic rule.'

'That's all I want', I said, 'to forget myself. But what if I can't? With me it's like when you can't get to sleep for ages, and all those instances when you have put your foot in it or taken a pratfall start going through your head, if you know what I mean.'

It turned out that Ed the yogi had no problem sleeping. That, too, is one of the beneficial effects of regular exercise.

'I thought', I said, 'that when I'm not thinking of anything, my soul will get bored and leave of its own accord. But it's not working, if only because I'm thinking about how I'm not supposed to think about anything, and so my soul happily stays where it is.'

'Zen Buddhists don't talk of the soul', said Ed. 'It smacks of religion. We prefer the term mind.'

I already know another rigorous scientist like that, I thought to myself.

5.1 Next came the episode with the police.

Before then my only first-hand experience of the police dated back to my student days, when I jumped off a moving tram right into the arms of a law enforcement officer lying in wait – their favourite stamping ground was near the National Theatre where the trams had to slow down, and it happened to be the closest point to the Bratislava *corso*. It was by no means a terrifying experience, the policeman just smiled and made me pay a ten-crown fine and that was it. Nevertheless, I admit that it gave me a fright to hear the doorbell ring and see Lienka flanked by two community support officers, even though I had no reason to feel frightened since I was well aware that their motto obliges them to protect and serve.

Traditionally, policemen come in two varieties, good cop and bad cop, but in this case I couldn't immediately tell which was which. If anything, they reminded me of Laurel and Hardy. 'We've brought your wife home', said the bigger one, the one with a good-natured double chin – Tibike – gently pushing Lienka towards me. She smiled sheepishly, like a child caught doing something naughty, and once in the flat she looked around the hallway as if she had never seen it before and expected to be introduced to it. Her hair was loose and dishevelled, as if she had been caught in a storm on her way home. I wasn't sure she recognised me: she didn't say a word. Maybe she was worried that her smile, which she held out in front of her like a shield, might also get ruffled.

'Come on in', I shouted over my shoulder, as I ushered her into the living room but when I returned a minute later, the men were still standing on the doorstep, saying they needed my consent to enter the flat. Afterwards I made some coffee in the kitchen and as they drank it standing up, they told me that on their rounds they sometimes stopped to check the IDs of a group of Gypsies who had been camping out in Šafárikovo Square or, since most of them didn't have any proof of identity, just to give them a scare or rough them up a bit. It was always the same group of shady characters who tended to gather there, and they had to be shown that someone was keeping an eye on them. As long as they didn't commit an offence, that was about all the police could do – they would never get a fine for a misdemeanour out of them and there would be little point chasing them away, since they would be back a minute later. So today, as they came to the park, they noticed this lady sitting on a bench in the park.

'She was just sitting there looking like she was crying', the younger one said, 'I mean, she wasn't bawling, but tears were streaming down her face. She was sitting right next to these homeless people and we wondered if they hadn't harmed her in some way. Insulted her or robbed her, you never know with these people.'

When the policemen began to talk to her she seemed startled and was generally confused, as if she didn't understand what they wanted. So they asked for her ID but she just stared at them in silence.

'She looked kind of stoned', the younger one said, giving me a searching look.

I shook my head. 'She's sick', I said. 'She has these fits sometimes.'

All I meant to do was firmly dispel his suspicions but as soon as I uttered the words 'she's sick', the full truth suddenly dawned on me for the first time. Sensei Ed might have called it a moment of enlightenment.

'Maybe it's her medication', Tibike remarked, 'perhaps she's on something strong, but she couldn't tell us where she lived, or remember her name. So we helped her find her ID, which has her address on it, and we thought we should bring her home, the condition she was in.'

'I don't know how to thank you', I said, as I saw them out.

When I returned to the living room, I didn't say: 'I'm glad you're back. I'm glad the policemen brought you back.' I just said: 'Thank God.'

She seemed to recognise the room and in its familiar embrace managed to pull herself together.

'I don't understand what they wanted from me', she said in her normal everyday voice, getting up from the armchair and heading for the wardrobe to take out her home clothes. 'They rummaged through my bag, are they allowed to do that?'

'They were helping you to find your ID', I replied. 'They had to find your address, you weren't able to tell them.'

I watched her getting changed, not in an immodest, pro-vocative way, but without any trace of shyness, as if she were alone in the room. What I saw before me was a body for everyday use, a body marked by the various tasks it had had to perform in the course of its life. It no longer even occurred to her that it was a commodity she could trade on the erotic stock market. I watched this body as if it were my own body except that I couldn't observe it at leisure like this, from a distance, and realised that if both our bodies had become worn out like this in harmony, side by side, they must now bear an outward resemblance to each other, like a pair of twins. Maybe even monozygotic ones. No, I didn't have a problem with the body itself, if only the soul that had met me at the front door had been the same. The only thing I held against her body was that it had started to produce some other, alien soul, one that I didn't recognise. I couldn't even think what to call it.

'Would you mind telling me', I said, 'what you were doing on that bench on Šafárikovo Square? What on earth made you go there?'

She pulled her t-shirt over her head and fixed me with an inquisitive look, as if trying to figure out if I was testing her. Eventually she decided she had figured it out and shrugged her shoulders.

'I suppose my legs hurt, so I sat down. Isn't that what benches are for?'

'We'll have to go and see a doctor', I said.

She gave me that inquisitive, almost hostile look again.

'Hang on', she said, 'what do you mean we should see a doctor? What for?'

2.p Regarding the question as to whether ants have a soul or not, I don't have a precise, scientific answer to offer. When I asked Lienka about it – in jest, of course – her only response was: What sort of question is that? It happened on one of those weekends when Katinka, or Miss D. as I called her, came to stay and Lienka probably suspected that I was mocking them both. She may have had a point. In any case, after putting Katinka to bed she told me off for giving the child silly ideas.

In fact, it was Katinka who had started the discussion, by asking whether ants also sweated. She was certain that moles did, because their fur is thick and when they burrow into the ground they must feel flushed because the inside of the Earth is hot. But ants have no fur, they are naked and tiny and may not even have anywhere to store their sweat. And what about when they crawl along the edge of a knife and cut themselves: do they bleed like human beings?

Her question might have implied that the institution didn't meet the highest health and safety standards – that sharp knives lay forgotten and scattered about the dining room, and that ants crawled over the tables – but I was loath to venture onto such delicate territory. Moles cropped up because of a cartoon Katinka had seen on TV, the ants had crawled in from God knows where and, to be frank, I was the one who had brought up the issue of their soul, although I didn't mean it entirely as a joke.

'I believe that ants are living beings, so they definitely have a soul', I said to Lienka later that evening when we were sitting on our own in the kitchen. If their bodies are capable of producing formic acid, what is to stop them from producing a soul? Why should it matter that they are tiny? After all, the human soul is also much larger than the human body, it is not a matter of physical size, and I am sure that the soul of a Pygmy is no smaller than that of a towering Maasai. Except that, when I picture an anthill, I'm not really sure if every ant is endowed with its own, individual soul or if they all share a single, collective mind. And how do they tell each other apart anyway? Does each ant have a proper name or a number? Or a number plate?

I pondered this for a moment. 'Have you noticed', I said, 'that when an ant is lugging a huge breadcrumb and other ants happen to be nearby, one will immediately rush to its aid while another might just pass it by? And when you take a closer look, you could swear that sometimes they are using their antennae to communicate. All this leads me to the conclusion that ants do have a soul, probably each of them an individual one. Take it from me.'

Lienka neither agreed nor disagreed. 'It seems that you and Katinka would actually get on really well', she announced as she got up from her chair. 'Let's go to bed', she said, 'she wakes up really early.'

3.f An avalanche is an accumulation of snow on the steep, bare slopes of a high mountain. When the balance of the mass of snow on an incline is disturbed, rapid movement is triggered, it gains speed and gathers more snow as it accelerates on its way to the bottom of the slope.

There are two common types of avalanche: a surface avalanche and a full-depth avalanche. In case of the former only one layer of snow slides over another layer, while in a full-depth one the entire snow cover, including the earth and rocks, slides over the ground. Both kinds of avalanche can be triggered by powder, wet or slab snow, including fine- or coarse-grained corn snow. The types of avalanche that occur most frequently in Slovakia are slab avalanches, formed of snow that has been deposited by the wind.

Avalanches come rolling down from the steepest mountains every year, converging on the protective tree-line defences and only rarely resulting in disaster on lower elevations. A well-known avalanche initiation point is Rybie (a locality in the village of Staré Hory in central Slovakia), below the eastern slopes of the Krížna Mountain, where ten fatalities were recorded on 17 March 1751 and eighteen on 6 February 1924.

Once an avalanche has been triggered it can't be stopped. Buildings at risk can be protected by deflecting the path of the avalanche or by the construction of splitting wedges.

These are the avalanches described in reference books. The kind of avalanche I'm talking about may resemble them in some respects and differ from them in others. However, what they undoubtedly have in common is that once they have been triggered they can't be stopped.

4.h 'Do you know what is the sound of one hand clapping?' I asked Štefan.

'In our academic world', he said, 'for example, when I gave a lecture at Marburg University or a paper at a conference in Brussels, applause is often expressed by banging one's hand on the desk top. So yes, in this sense, that would be the sound of one hand clapping.'

He seems to know everything there is to know about the academic world.

'Let me put it differently', I said. 'If what you did with one hand wasn't banging but clapping, would you hear the sound?'

He glanced at me to check that I wasn't taking the mickey. 'Hardly', he said. 'There wouldn't be a sound to hear.'

'But Zen Buddhists can hear it, you see', I said. 'I'm serious.'

Štefan thinks the world is full of crackpots but I didn't let him off so easily. I explained how it works: Zen Buddhists believe that sound exists all the time, regardless of applause, otherwise we couldn't hear someone clapping their hands, because where would the sound be coming from? If you clap with one hand, it's your hand that is really the sound and a Zen Buddhist can hear it. But if you try too hard and prick up your ears, you won't.

'And you can make head or tail of this nonsense?' he asked.

'Not entirely', I replied. 'For example, I can just about understand that when you set out to paint something, the picture already exists the moment you dip the brush in the paint. This is because you already have an idea of the picture in your head. But it's beyond me that you need to be absolutely enlightened in order to reach absolute enlightenment. What do you need absolute enlightenment for if you're already absolutely enlightened?

To achieve absolute enlightenment squared? But wouldn't such enlightenment squared be detrimental to your health, like when you get a double dose of radiation from an X-ray machine? You're the scientist, maybe you can advise me.'

'The only advice I can give you', said Štefan, 'is to forget all these ravings and that guru of yours as soon as you can.'

'Guru is what they're called in India. The Japanese as well as the American Zen Buddhists call their masters sensei.'

'Guru, sensei', Štefan rolled his eyes, 'same difference.' And when he learned that sensei Ed trained in California, he rolled his eyes again. California! He thinks the climate in California is conducive to all these kinds of hare-brained movements: hippies, psychedelics, tantrists, holotropists and every other sort of ists. Surely it is no accident that the dream factory was also spawned in California. The ideal place for fantasists.

'How long did this oriental dance teacher actually spend in America?' he asked. 'Two years? Well, then it's obvious that in his case the American dream has failed. He has come back, so obviously he didn't make it there.'

Štefan believes that every newspaper vendor, waiter or kitchen porter in the United States dreams that a brilliant future awaits them and that one day they will be rich and famous. Some do succeed, and their stories are passed around, encouraging other fantasists. And because of this American dream the US is considered the land of limitless opportunity. And those who don't make it will clutch at any kind of dubious movement or religion, such as Zen Buddhism.

'Here in Central Europe we've been raised on other stories', he said, 'ones without a Hollywood-style happy ending. Typical Central Europeans anticipate a shipwreck from the word go, and their only concern is to make sure they founder in a dignified way, preferably on a big ship and not far from the shore where an audience can see them. And a person blessed with such healthy scepticism, who has come to accept failure in advance, won't be attracted to or fall for any oriental phantasmagorias.'

A veritable lecture. I nearly applauded Štefan with one hand, but he wouldn't have heard the applause anyway.

'I'm warning you', he said eventually, 'you're on a slippery slope and you'll step on some shit before you know it.'

'Don't worry', I said, 'I just need something to keep myself occupied. I'll never be a Buddhist because I can't cross my legs. But as a rigorous scientist, maybe you can tell me what clavicular breathing is?'

2.9 I didn't tell Štefan or Ed, but I didn't actually take Zen Buddhism seriously. You just can't. If the purpose of the body is to produce the soul then without a soul it loses its purpose, and what can one do about that? I don't believe that the soul is a whim of nature, like the appendix, and that we can remove it when it becomes painful without lasting consequences. I already know that there are times when we can cope only by affecting indifference but that was no reason to get rid of my soul, all I wanted to achieve through the spiritual exercise was to make it more resistant to disease. The disease called life.

I imagined – perhaps partly influenced by Ed's explanation – that Buddhist meditation was akin to a kung-fu bout, in which a moment of motionless concentration is followed by a crushing blow, and that enlightenment, too, was a sudden explosion of awareness, one that strikes like lightning from a clear sky. Maybe I have the wrong idea of the martial arts and maybe it isn't just my body but also my soul that is too old for this kind of exercise; either way, there was no explosion.

I also assumed that if I managed to forget myself there would be more room left for others, but what kind of forgetting is it if it is still me who is thinking about these others? I can't just be peeled off them, like the skin from an orange.

And to be completely honest, I can't bring myself to believe that a man who had once applied all his ingenuity to ripping off his friends by swapping razor blade packets for Hagenbeck pictures would find fulfilment by letting his completely white-washed soul dissolve in the universe. How does that square with the successful fitness centre business he started in Slovakia? Isn't that a textbook example of dualism?

Zen Buddhism is nothing but snowflakes that have come drifting on the wind from far away, so light and tiny that it might be just the air shimmering. Maniwaki. Or maybe Petawawa?

1.0 I found it hard to come up with a name for her new soul. When it became unavoidable, I started to address her body, which seemed unchanged except for the vacant face; I told myself that her buttocks, even if now at half-mast, were still attractive, but that would be taking things out of context. I called her Magdaléna, that was the name of the body shown in her ID, and this vast semi-detached name also seemed to provide more space for her unanchored soul. It seemed to allow her to leap from Magda to Léna as and when needed, like a movie baddie leaping from a galloping horse onto a speeding train. The baddie Ďuriačik didn't manage to jump across into Baumgartner like this, he fell under the wheels. A date for a court hearing hadn't yet been set but he was facing a term of imprisonment of one to ten years under Article 249.

She didn't even notice the change of name. Or at least she didn't let on if she did.

5.j Medical professionals don't use the unscientific term soul. They have no reason to, as their focus is exclusively on the body. Our neurologist spoke of an organic process in the brain, which confused me at first because until then I had been under the impression that everything that was organic was good.

To assist him in this conversation he invited two scary look-ing underlings by the name of Morbus I and Morbus II – their surnames are not important since the doctor himself hadn't yet decided which one was the better fit for her, and they resembled each other like a pair of twins. Step-twins. He said that at her age this wasn't likely to be senile dementia, it was too early for that.

He also told me that the process was irreversible and the most that current medical science could do was slow it down. I don't know what he said to Magdaléna, I was waiting in the corridor while he talked to her so as not to distract her with my pres-ence, but she came out of the surgery looking happy, her cheeks flushed with joy. Then the neurologist called me in for a word.

'Well?' she asked me when I was back in the corridor. 'How did you do? Did you manage to remember all the pictures?'

'Not all of them', I replied cautiously because the doctor hadn't mentioned any picture tests to me and I didn't know how well she had done. I didn't want her to feel any unnecessary concern or to arouse her suspicions.

'I did really well', she said, her face still flushed and beaming. 'I even managed to draw most of them.'

2.r In summer time my soul wears loose underpants. Although they are popularly known as boxer shorts, I must say that they don't make my soul look like a boxer at all. Rather, it looks like a scaredy-cat, frightened of the slightest draught. But whether I like it or not, it is an expression of its free, genuine will and I have to accept that.

In America, as Štefan says, schoolchildren are not taught joined-up writing. Instead, they are taught a script made up of small circles and short straight sticks, sometimes called 'ball and stick' writing. This trend will no doubt soon infiltrate our schools as well, for how could we afford to lag behind the rest of the world? But how much of a unique soul can you fit into a short straight stick? How genuinely and accurately can it be expressed within these constraints? Before we know it, ball and stick writing itself will be driven to extinction by keyboards that make no allowance for the existence of the soul. It would just prevent the free flow of communication.

Štefan's grandfather Tibike used to have his boots made to measure by a shoemaker. They were tailored exactly to the size of his body and soul because the bootmaker would not only carefully measure every curve of his big toe but also try to satisfy his customer's idea of what should be the colour of the leather, the height of the shaft and the thickness of the lining. The boots were not cheap but they were unique, they had Tibike's name written all over them, so to speak, and they would last thirty years. Štefan's father, on the other hand, used to buy shoes mass-produced by the Baťa factory. They were much cheaper but the name written on them was Baťa's, and his foot and soul needed to adjust to them. And there was a lot of adjusting for them to do, because these shoes had a short lifespan and fashion kept changing. I suppose it was Henry Ford who started this trend by offering his customers affordable cars in any colour as long as it was black. With this kind of novelty, who gives a damn about colour?

Štefan would say that there are too many of us around for everyone to have shoes made to measure, many people wouldn't be able to afford them and would be reduced to going barefoot. There is certainly something to this, the world is full of people who go barefoot as it is. But the shoes as such are not really the point. The point is that once the manufacturers decided to get rid of half sizes, we, too, gave up our half-sized feet – we can try on the shoes before buying them and at the end of the day a pair that's half a size too big or too small represents good value. We give in, completely unaware of the consequences. Metaphorically speaking, mass-produced footwear generates mass-produced bodies and mass-produced bodies will sooner or later start to generate mass-produced souls. This makes life easier and more comfortable all round. The more the merrier, as they say, and from the point of view of society mass-produced people are fine because they are easier to deal with. They are easier to classify for statistical purposes.

But Štefan isn't keen on the metaphorical way of speaking. 'Whether you're wearing boots made to measure or mass-produced shoes, your feet will always smell the same. And even if you wrapped them in a hundred souls, it wouldn't make them smell of daisies.'

Soul is an artificially inflated, ostentatious word and that is why Štefan can't stand it. He believes we are dealing with ordinary physiological processes of the human body and we are wrong to imagine that, by referring to them as the soul, we can elevate a person to nobler status. From a creature to a being. The Menominee may have been able to accommodate this term in their supernatural world view but it sounds false when uttered by a modern man.

'I don't claim to be a modern man', I said, 'but I promise never again to utter the word in your presence.'

'Never mind me', said Štefan shrugging his shoulders, 'forget about me. The main thing is that you banish this idea from your own head.'

As usual, he had got hold of the wrong end of the stick. I was only joking.

5.k An avalanche is an irreversible process. Once it has been set in motion it is unstoppable. All science can do is help slow it down, although I get the impression that science actually makes it accelerate. It keeps reminding us that we are misguided and in this misguided and bewildered state we are no longer sure what to think. We will swallow anything as long as it hasn't passed its sell-by date.

I wouldn't bring love into this. Not that it doesn't fit in here but because it introduces an element of volatility. There is no warranty for love and once the avalanche has been set in motion it will come hurtling down, heedless of love. After all, the reason love is such a popular word is that anyone can make it mean whatever they like. Maybe we should talk of compassion instead.

I kept addressing her body as Magdaléna but for a brief while I found a private, secret name for her soul. When I mentioned to the doctor that she had problems signing her name at the post office, he informed me that this was a symptom of the disease – the patient may forget how to write. The technical term is agraphia. The first time I heard this it didn't register, but after one particular domestic clash this Russian-sounding name suddenly seemed to suit her new, fickle and moodily oscillating soul, the vast Russian soul, if you will. Agraphia Nikolayevna could easily be the name of the heroine of Dostoevsky's *The Idiot*, I thought. I know it wasn't a nice thing to say but it helped me deal with the fit of rage that came over me at that moment. Even though we had seen the doctor I hadn't yet managed to turn on that switch in my brain and shunt Magdaléna onto a side track – what bewildered me was that her confused states alternated with clear-headed or, to use the neurologist's technical term lucid, periods. To put it bluntly, I discerned a clear ulterior motive in her behaviour: to spite me.

Dragging love into this is tricky because love, just like smooth muscle, isn't under the control of our will. Not that it doesn't exist, but at a certain moment it suddenly disappears. The clash I mentioned earlier, if I may call it that, happened over a dish of pasta with bolognaise sauce. When I put the plate in front of Magdaléna, she pushed it away so violently that she sent a few little spirals flying onto the table and the tomato sauce left red stains on the tablecloth.

'How many times have I told you I don't like pasta', she said, 'can't you get it into your head? Or are you doing this out of spite?'

That's how Agraphia was born – I have left out the patronymic because Agraphia Ladislavovna doesn't sound particularly Dostoevskian. I was taken aback by this outburst, as until then she had always appreciated the fact that I had taken over kitchen duties and would eat pasta just like any other dishes in my limited culinary repertoire, sometimes with relish, almost greedily, at other times forcing it down indifferently, as if her thoughts had wandered somewhere far from the table. Although I hadn't yet got used to it, I had already noticed that she would sometimes treat me with a kind of sly, thinly disguised hostility. The prickly look she gave me was in sharp contrast to the childlike trustfulness with which she usually accepted my advice and guidance – for instance, that she ought to put on tights and a cardigan because it had turned chilly, or that she should check that all the gas rings had been turned off before leaving the kitchen. She didn't hesitate to consult me on issues such as how long it was likely to keep raining, or how much sugar she should put in her coffee, as if she no longer trusted her own taste buds.

It was around this time that Alica first made an appearance. She walked into our life with little fuss and with no explanation, without introducing herself properly. On that day, Agraphia had spent the entire morning opening all the drawers of the wardrobe and sideboard and rummaging about in them.

'You haven't taken my gold earrings by any chance?' she asked eventually, crouching over the contents of the bottom drawer laid out on the rug. 'I can't find them anywhere.'

'No', I said, taken aback. 'What would I do with them? I don't wear earrings.'

'How would I know what you'd do with them', she said. 'Who knows, perhaps sell them for the gold? The thing is, they were a keepsake, a present from Alica.'

To be honest, I had no clue what earrings she was talking about. I remembered vaguely that someone had once mentioned a pair of golden earrings her godparents had given her but I wasn't really sure. Either way, it wasn't just that I had never worn earrings, she had never worn them either – in fact, she had never had her ears pierced. In her student days she sometimes wore clip-ons but once they went out of fashion it wasn't worth keeping cheap trinkets of that kind.

No, I knew nothing of her earrings or of Alica. The earrings would soon be forgotten, never to be mentioned again, but Alica stayed with us. When I asked who she was, Agraphia replied with an enigmatic smile: 'A friend of mine, but you don't know her.'

That was certainly true.

4.i Štefan was my twin, albeit only a step-twin, but he was still capable of surprising me. One day, when I dropped by his office out of the blue, he handed me a large, heavy book wrapped in flowery gift paper without saying a word.

'What's up?' I asked. 'What's got into you, it's not my birthday or name-day today.'

'Oh, it's just something that caught my eye in a bookshop', he replied. 'It was sitting on a shelf next to books on linguistics. It made me think of you straight away and I knew you would appreciate it. So Irenka and I decided to club together and get you a present.'

Sitting at her small desk, Irenka – just like the girl in the Grimm Brothers' fairy tale, who came to see the king wrapped in a fishnet – neither watched nor did not watch the solemn handover. She seemed to blush a little but then again, it is quite dark in Štefan's cubbyhole.

'Thank you, Irenka', I said, unwrapping the book. I didn't thank Štefan although I didn't believe for a moment that he could be so stingy as to dip into the PhD student's miserable grant. I concluded that this was his way of subtly signalling her official position. Girlfriend number... well, there wasn't enough time to work it out. What a clever solution, you rascal, I thought, you didn't have to go very far, Irenka freshened the air for you right here at your place of work.

We live in a free country nowadays and all sorts of odd books get published. This one, as I discovered when I unwrapped it, was a collection of glossy photographs of women's buttocks. Some had been taken out of context, others needed an immediate or overall context but all of them were a joy to behold – a shapely rear is the most beautiful part of a woman's anatomy. What bothered me was that I wasn't sure what sort of stories Štefan had told Irenka as they were buying the book, so I decided to leave the detailed inspection of the gift until later.

'It's the buttock worshipper's bible', said Štefan, 'one of those new-fangled Californian sects. But I think it can also provide inspiration for Buddhist meditation.'

'Well, these bottoms certainly existed long before the photographer released the shutter', I replied, 'and that's in line with the teachings of Buddhism. It's true-blue Catholics like you who are out of luck, God will bring you to book on Judgement Day for looking at pictures like these.'

'Don't drag God into this', Štefan said, 'that's too big a shoe for me, it will fall off my foot. Catholic or not, I'm basically a decent person and decent people don't look at strangers' bottoms. I'm chaste, if you know the meaning of that word.'

Coming from him I could only treat this as a joke and after giving it some thought I concluded that the gift itself was just his clumsy attempt at wit. Is it possible that the distinguished scholar has, in middle age, finally dared to venture onto the slippery slope of humour? I would have liked to browse the photographs with him so he could show me which of the bottoms most resembled Irenka's but it wasn't appropriate to do so in her presence.

When I closed the book, I noticed the price on the back cover: 40 euros. That must have been quite a painful blow to Štefan's wallet.

'I have another special word for you', I said, by way of compensation for his pains, 'it may be new to you.'

Štefan gave me a suspicious look.

'*Blus*', I said. 'Ring any bells?'

Štefan said nothing and waited for me to continue. Irenka was the only one to respond. '*Blus*?' she asked. 'I don't think we've come across that one before.'

'*Blus*', I repeated. 'Remember *blosa*? The white blaze on the forehead of domestic cattle? Well, *blus* is a black mark, a blob, on a human forehead.'

'*Blus*?' With a soft *l*?' Irenka swivelled her chair towards the computer. 'Should I enter it straight into the database?' she asked Štefan.

He shook his head. 'Don't enter anything', he said. 'And remember never to take this man seriously, he's a buffoon. He is a *flus*, a black mark or gob of spit, on the forehead of humanity.'

Even in the weak light coming from the window it was now obvious that Irenka was blushing. But I think she was embarrassed less for herself than for those two childish middle-aged men.

It isn't easy to be a budding female scholar in this world, especially if your supervisor suddenly tries to be witty.

1·p As I have said before, it wasn't nice of me to call her Agraphia. Initially I was slightly ashamed about this act of silent revenge. I felt guilty about the fact that it made me feel better. But thinking about it later, as I sat cross-legged, I experienced a moment of enlightenment. It was only partial and vague, as you might expect when musing, but it made me realise that the name Agraphia wasn't really a slur. Her transformation was undeniable, she was no longer Duška nor Lienka, and yet

I didn't call this new persona Morbus I or Morbus II, as a neurologist might have done. I didn't regard her solely as a hollow, portable casing for disease. The name Agraphia still granted her recognition as a unique human being with a soul, even if a Russian one, so vast that its limits were nowhere to be seen.

Agraphia! I would leave love out of it, as Agraphia was moving steadily away from me. But now I knew why the Menominee respect mad people, and I had come to share their respect for them. A rigorous scientist like Štefan would perhaps have called it awe.

2.8 The word love is so popular because anyone is free to make it mean whatever they like – some might see it as a fusion of bodies, others as a fusion of souls. It is the latter who usually end up disappointed. If we assume that the human soul is unique (though that is something Štefan the scientist would never admit) this outcome is logical and inevitable. For a fusion to occur the person in question has to reverse out of their own soul at least a little bit to make room for the other, and it's not something you can keep doing without suffering the consequences. Few people would want to remain fused with a void for very long, it isn't much fun. But there are moments when two souls, even if travelling in opposite directions, pass each other and exchange a friendly wave, like tram drivers who work the same route. Now I realise that all one can expect of love are these precious, fleeting moments of intimacy.

But what if one of the drivers is suddenly assigned a different route?

5.1 Exercise, exercise, exercise, was the doctors' advice in true Leninist style. Exercising the memory is one way of slowing down the decline.

Lienka was brighter than me. This claim is not based on IQ tests, as neither of us has taken any and if we had, I might have scored higher because I am better at solving logical tasks, but that is irrelevant. I think she was brighter because she used to see things from a perspective that would never have occurred to me. Metaphorically speaking, where I would have been happy to state that it was raining, she would immediately remark that this was the kind of light rain that made children grow, that there would be less dust in the street now that it had had a nice sprinkling, or that once the sun peeped out from behind that cloud we would see a rainbow – but I'm just wasting time here, I can't replicate these unexpected associations of hers. Just imagine what the people of, say, Niger in Africa, would give to be blessed with rain like this! Štefan, who is not keen on metaphorical ways of speaking, would say that her world had a more varied texture, although coming from him this wouldn't have been unalloyed praise because the purpose of science is to prise the essence out of a cluster of facts and eliminate marginal phenomena from the thought process.

But now it was Agraphia we were dealing with. If Agraphia had taken any notice of the rain, she would have said, at most, that it had rained just like this that time she and Alica went for a swim at the Zlaté Piesky lake. In fact, I was the one who was with her that Sunday when we were caught out by a summer storm at Zlaté Piesky, but whenever I tried to exercise her memory by reminding her of the things we had experienced together, the results would be unexpected. For example, I asked her if she remembered where and when we had our first kiss, and when she said nothing for a long time, I prompted her and said it was at the Hviezda cinema – still nothing – where we had gone to see *Rocco and His Brothers*. She stared in silence at a point in the middle distance and suddenly, as if she hadn't heard what I said, declared that she remembered the film very well because she went to see it with Alica three times, once at the amphitheatre on Castle Hill, and she recalled that they had to walk back and since Alica, who lived further away, was scared of the dark,

93

Lienka walked her home. Actually, I think it was Agraphia who walked her home on that particular occasion, but I thought it wiser not to tell her that this was what I suspected.

The problem was that in the rare moments when Agraphia admitted there was something wrong with her, she treated her illness like a leg that had gone numb and assumed it was something she could walk off. As a matter of fact, I have no idea what she was thinking, but this was how she behaved. And so I would disguise these exercises: for example, I would write down ten random numbers on a piece of paper and suggest that we have a competition to see which of us would remember more of them. But there was no point pretending that I couldn't manage more than six numbers since, on the second attempt, she declared suspiciously: 'You're testing me', and refused to continue. Maybe she was offended that I was trying tricks on her that she had used on her disabled charges, or maybe she was missing her reward of a *Marína* biscuit. Sometimes we would do crossword puzzles – ostensibly together, I would take one clue, she the next – but after spending five minutes fruitlessly trying to come up with the name of an Italian river, two letters, she flung her pencil away and said she had never liked crosswords and couldn't see why she should waste her time on them now. I don't want to drag love into it, but if the choice was between losing her trust or the memory gymnastics, I wouldn't hesitate which one to pick. So in the end all that was left were exercises recommended by the psychiatrist to be carried out under professional supervision at the care centre. I don't know what exactly they did there, she either didn't want to explain or couldn't, but when I came to collect her three hours later she greeted me with the words: 'There you are, at last. Don't ever bring me here again, this place is full of weird people, some don't even seem to know their own name.'

But I kept taking her to spend time with these weird people. After all, she didn't know that her name was Agraphia either.

4.j 'How are you doing, you *kopirdan*, you bastard child you, still *komprding* Irenka?' I said to Štefan. I thought he would appreciate the fact that I had committed these words to memory but he was not amused. He said Irenka wasn't around today, she had gone – at this point he involuntarily raised his eyes to the ceiling – gliding. 'It's her hobby, gliding. The girl's crazy', he said with admiration.

'I told you she's a crow', I replied, 'no wonder she goes flying.'

Štefan can't understand this since he's not keen on flying. He is scared. Even now that travelling has become so much easier, he hasn't been back to America although his university had invited him to come and promote his book. But to get to America you have to fly and it's a long haul. On top of that now there is the terrorist threat, the security checks and all the hassle at the airports, which is enough to put off even travellers less enthusiastic than he is.

Štefan won't admit this, of course, his excuse is that he doesn't feel like going, that all that American hustle and bustle is not his cup of tea. His dislike of metaphors notwithstanding, he said that New York resembles a quarry that has been ravaged by termites and anyway it is obvious that most American cities lack history, that they hadn't evolved slowly and organically but rather shot up overnight, as if built with Lego bricks by a giant without any imagination. Europeans miss their picturesque little alleyways and quiet, secluded corners, cosy little cafés and tiny family-run shops, fountains with small statues of saints, and so on – I noted with interest how many diminutives he used in his description. As if the main problem with America was that everything there was oversized.

Towards the end of his American sojourn in the late 1960s Štefan made a two-week trip around the United States, so he knows what he is talking about. He claims there are only two cities in the entire US where he could live, San Francisco and

New Orleans. These haven't been blighted by this cancerous growth, have retained their human scale, enjoying a beautiful location on the coast and boast European-style neighbourhoods. And, perhaps symptomatically, both are under mortal threat: San Francisco is situated on a tectonic fault where a catastrophic earthquake might occur at any moment, like the one that struck the city in 1906, when a large part of it was destroyed by tremors and fires, while the threat to New Orleans was recently illustrated when hurricane Katrina smashed the levees, and the entire city was flooded. Štefan believes there is something European about this, too, people who live with the sword of Damocles hanging above their heads have a different attitude to life, they know how to savour its small pleasures instead of mindlessly chasing the mirage of success.

Although this was just an impromptu lecture, made up on the spur of the moment, it was quite instructive – I discovered what kind of things a scientist will come up with just to avoid admitting to his fear of flying.

'We also have a city like that', I said, 'San Francisco and New Orleans rolled into one. Komárno has also suffered a few earthquakes, I remember one of them made the glasses rattle in the cupboard in our house as far away as Bratislava, to say nothing of the many occasions Komárno has been inundated by the Danube. You'd be hard pressed to find anyone there mindlessly chasing the mirage of success. People of that ilk left long ago.'

Štefan was unfazed. Earthquake, fire, flood – he thinks that regardless of the current state of knowledge people are still basically helpless against the elements.

'You're right', I replied. 'But it's not fire or water that will wipe us out, we'll get snowed under. Maybe the only person who will survive is your Irenka, because she can fly.'

Štefan's only response to this was *flus*.

5.m I thought … actually, I don't know what I thought. Desperation is the mother of desperate ideas. I bought myself a mouth organ, one of those little things that fit into the palm of your hand. I'm not musical at all and I don't read music either, but that's beside the point. It's not the musical performance that matters, it is the act of playing *per se*, the fact that you get up and make a determined effort to comfort another person, hoping against hope that it will work, however badly you play. You are, in a word, a *futrangoš*, a flibbertigibbet.

I wouldn't go on about love in this context. The one being who felt unconditional love for Lienka was Kora, who had accompanied her every movement with loving eyes. But both Kora and Lienka are long gone. One day, when Agraphia was standing by the window again, lost in thought, gazing at the grey wall of the block of flats opposite, I stood behind her and put my arms around her shoulders. Love, as people usually imagine it, is a mutually profitable affair – one person longs for an embrace, the other longs to be embraced, and when the embrace happens it makes both of them happy. This was a different kind of love. I didn't expect to gain anything from embracing her; I didn't long to embrace her, I just wanted to comfort her. To show her that I was there for her, that she could lean her back against me, as against a tiled stove, to keep warm. But when she felt the touch of my hands, Agraphia recoiled, turned round and said: 'Do you mind, sir?!'

As for the mouth organ, I eventually mastered … actually, I just imagined that I mastered, two or three well-known folk songs: the one about rain, *Prší prší*, then the one about a whirl-pool, *Tam okolo Levoči*, and *Hej, kamaráti moji, tu ma nenechajte*, Hey, my friends, don't leave me here – that one in particular was really hard work. I couldn't tell whether the song meant anything to Agraphia, or even if she recognised it in my rendition. As she sat lost in the folds of the armchair, I would come up to her, mouth organ at the ready, and begin to play, but all she would do was raise her eyebrows in surprise or perhaps in horror. Unlike me, she has an ear for music. In the end, I would just improvise, randomly producing notes for a while, that's all there was to it, until we both burst out laughing: I would always be the first to laugh so she wouldn't need to worry that I might be offended by her laughter. Perhaps Agraphia didn't even know what she was laughing at, and just joined in.

Call it mood swings if you like. Sometimes she would lock herself in the bathroom and spend a full hour there dressing up and putting on her make-up. 'Going out?' I would ask but she never deigned to reply. Perhaps she had no explanation, she was just going through old routines on a whim. Most of the time, however, she neglected her appearance. She would forget to comb her hair and sometimes I had to trick her into the bathtub, with bath salts from the Dead Sea or a new bath foam. I even bought her a yellow plastic duck, turning it into a joke. I had never before been involved with her body in this kind of intimate way. She had no inhibitions in my presence, like a small child she didn't resist when I washed her, as if her body were a piece of luggage she had deposited in a locker because it was in the way and she now no longer had to worry about it. As if she had dismissed it from her mind for good.

As for her soul, things were different. She made sure it was well hidden from me and when I tried to seek it out, she never prompted me by saying 'getting warmer' or 'getting colder', merely smiling faintly at my efforts. Nevertheless, I had no doubt that she did have a soul, and that it wasn't simply her original soul, broken and sick, but a brand new one, completely different. I had respect for this soul, the more so for not understanding it. Perhaps I was slightly scared of it, because, what if… I would say to myself. What if what we regard as illness is, in fact, a sign of superior health? What if she has an additional gene, one the rest of us lack in our genetic make-up? What if she is endowed with the ability to see, or at least to intuit, the future and has already started to make preparations for it? It wouldn't be the first time that a genius was considered a lunatic, since it is not easy, indeed it is impossible, to draw a sharp line between the two. Maybe which of the two we opt for is purely a matter of personal choice.

It was around this time that in my mind I started calling Agraphia by another name, Eugénia.

3.g You don't need Zen Buddhism to experience a moment of enlightenment. In our Christian religion, too, we are familiar with the revelation or, to use a technical term from ancient Greek, epiphany. This is supposed to be the manifestation of a higher, divine power but those of us who have little time for God or think he has feet of clay perceive it as a sudden falling of the scales from our eyes. A flash of recognition. You don't have to sit cross-legged or empty your mind, lightning can strike at any time, in any state or posture - while crossing the street, shopping for acacia honey at the market, enjoying a glass of wine in a bar, or dangling head down from a trapeze.

When I said as much to Edo – by way of goodbye or explanation of why I was not going to carry on with the exercises – he didn't protest too much. He must have written me off as an unpromising pupil because I raised too many objections right from the start.

'Suit yourself', he said, 'but you're making a mistake. Those Christian revelations of yours have nothing to do with spiritual enlightenment, they're just delusions. Believe me, I know something about that, I also used to go to church. Some kids in a spa town somewhere in France imagined they had a vision of the Virgin Mary and people made a huge fuss about it.'

'You mean Lourdes?' I asked. 'There was no spa there at the time, that came only after the visions. Along with the miraculous healing water. And the place where some kids saw the Virgin Mary was Portugal, but there's no spa there.'

'Makes no difference', he said. 'It's always kids. Not long ago there was also that case in Yugoslavia, or whatever the country is called these days. It's always kids and always the Virgin Mary. Isn't that a coincidence? Ever heard of a normal sensible adult coming across an apparition of, say, St Peter or the Archangel Gabriel? Children's fantasies, if you ask me, if not out-and-out fraud.'

'Perhaps it's because the Virgin Mary is fond of children', I said. 'St Peter is a grouchy old codger, they would get on his nerves, and besides, he's got other things to worry about. He has to guard the pearly gates to make sure the wrong kind of people don't get into heaven. And as for Gabriel, if he appeared to kids with that flaming sword of his they'd be so scared they'd go straight off to meet their maker and nobody would ever learn of the miracle.'

'Let me tell you something about that holy water', Ed responded. 'There's this woman in my class, in her fifties maybe, she was paralysed after a car accident. She could only manage a couple of steps around her flat on crutches, so she joined a pilgrimage to this spa, splashed about in the holy water but there was no miracle. And you should see her now, after doing the exercises for less than a year! She still needs a walking stick because she has a bit of a limp, but soon she won't need that either. And she's a grown woman, no innocent child, and she didn't need a vision of the Virgin Mary. All she's done is practise yoga regularly and conscientiously.'

'Maybe she glimpsed Buddha in a moment of absolute enlightenment', I said. 'Either way, as the Bible says, she has been healed by her faith. But in my case the outcome would be the exact opposite, I have no faith in the healing process and if I sat cross-legged for another month I would wind up needing those crutches.'

It turned out that Buddha never makes an appearance. Buddha, Ed claimed, is somewhere inside us, every one of us is a kind of Buddha-carrier, and the whole point of meditation is to find him and bring him to life. An interesting theory, the only fly in the ointment being that if Buddha resembles his statues even a little, he would never fit inside me.

To be honest, I feel no hankering for the Buddha or the Virgin Mary to appear to me, it's too late for miracles now. I can already hear the grass grow, and soon it will be buried under an avalanche. Obviously, I fear that moment, as it will be my first avalanche, but at the same time I do pin some hopes on it. I hope that at that instant – as people who have been on the brink of death report – my whole life will flash before me and that this accelerated, condensed summary will reveal to me what all this has been about and what the purpose of my life was. Metaphorically speaking, I hope to find out what purpose has been served by my soul.

This is the only revelation, the only absolute enlightenment I crave, and I don't care whether I'm sitting cross-legged when it happens or ramrod-straight from head to heel.

5.n Desperate ideas, every single one of them. For example, I was wondering why it didn't work out with the mouth organ as I had hoped, why my playing didn't exude impish joy, like the surgeon's whistling, which, let's face it, wasn't really up to concert standard either, how it was that the notes he played dispersed around the surgery like schoolchildren during their break, whereas mine stayed firmly stuck in the dunces' corner. Then I worked out what the difference between us was: while music flowed freely from him, I had to force it out of myself. I wanted to misuse music as a treatment, but I'm not a good liar and she caught me out. One should leave medical treatment to doctors, it is their job and they are better at it. And Eugénia doesn't want to be treated anyway, she is convinced that she is in good health, and as far as she is concerned we are the ones who are sick and retarded. She is already one step ahead of us, the avalanche is beginning to bury her and she is doing everything she can not to be dragged down by us, the unenlightened, us who have no inkling.

That's all there is to it, this is what I think now. For what else am I to think? And yet how long it took me to admit this! How I resisted! Take the Tatras, for example, one of my most desperate ideas. Lienka and I never had a proper honeymoon, I married in uniform while on military service and the two days' leave wasn't long enough to go anywhere. Two years later, to make up for it, Lienka's parents booked us into the Grand Hotel in Starý Smokovec for a weekend, a luxury this young couple could never afford. Personally, I wouldn't have picked the High Tatras, I'm not into mountain climbing, and nature, confined as it is to the cage of a national park, strikes me as rather tame and scruffy. But you don't look a gift horse in the mouth, even if some of its teeth are missing; we gratefully accepted the gift and, Tatras or no Tatras, spent three lovely winter days together.

So now I had this idea ... even after all my unsuccessful attempts to summon up the ghosts of the past I naïvely assumed that our first trip, our semi-honeymoon, might still lie slumbering somewhere in the recesses of her memory and could be reawakened by the familiar scenery. With my and God's help. To be honest, I couldn't recall much of the trip myself but I thought that if we both repeated the mantra 'remember when ...' this joint effort might flush some memories out of their hiding places and kick-start Eugénia's seized-up memory. I was hoping ... God knows what I was hoping for, people say that hope dies last – and, I might add, it is also born first, often so prematurely that it is more like a miscarriage. This time it was summer rather than winter and I went to the Tatras in the company of Agraphia rather than Eugénia.

As far as her face was concerned Lienka left me long ago. She had three different masks to cover up the blankness. The most common one was a vague, frozen smile with which she silently accepted everything happening around her, as if from behind a low stone parapet. The smile seemed to be telling me: I understand what you're trying to do but let me reserve judgment. The second mask was an expression that might best be described as that of someone who has unexpectedly burned her lips on hot coffee; she would soon recover from the shock and powder it over with a smile. And the third mask was a vacant gaze, directed at something distant within her, the gaze of a character who is performing on a different stage and in a completely different play from all those around her. She wore it mainly when she thought nobody was watching her, and perhaps it wasn't really a mask at all, simply her genuine, true new face.

There had been some warning signs earlier but I chose to ignore them. When I first mentioned the trip to the Tatras, she smiled demurely – of course, of course, I know, the Tatras – but as I did her packing she kept trying to stuff her evening gowns and heels into the suitcase. I patiently explained that what she would need in the mountains was a windcheater and walking boots – she nodded with a smile, only to come back with a frilly white blouse, one that she had probably last worn to dancing lessons. On the train she was silent for a long time, every now and then casting a worried look at the countryside until, finally, somewhere around Považská Bystrica, she asked softly and timidly: 'Where are we going?' 'To the Tatras, we're going on an outing, remember?' I replied. She nodded eagerly, still with a slightly frightened smile. Once we had checked into the Park Hotel, she stood for a while in the middle of our room looking lost, then took a few cautious steps towards the bed, patted the pillow, switched on the lamp on the bedside table, peered into the bathroom with its shower cubicle, and turned to me with the question: 'Is this where we're going to live now?' And without waiting for a reply, she went on: 'Where's the kitchen then?'

It could have been worse. The first couple of days I could still fool myself that I was there with Eugénia. She dutifully put on her walking boots and windcheater and came with me to the funicular station at Hrebienok. Once there, she listened in silence while I repeated the mantra – 'Remember how we went down the toboggan run?' – just nodding whenever I gave her an expectant glance. She looked at me respectfully and deferentially, as you might at the mountain guide on whom you rely when you arrive in an unfamiliar place, because he knows his way around. As for the memories, she listened to mine with courteous interest, as if I were telling her about my adventures on a holiday in some faraway, exotic land, without throwing in a single word from her own store of memories because – what else was I to think –she had never been lucky enough to visit such parts.

A turning point came when we took the train to the tarn of Štrbské pleso. She trailed one step behind me as we walked along the narrow path around the lake, looking at three or four little boats which from afar looked like ducks sitting on the water. A family with two children in orange life-jackets could be made out in the nearest boat. I stopped, turned to her and nodded in the direction of the water.

'Isn't it incredible', I said, 'that there was a time when this lake was completely frozen over and we could walk across to the far side? Do you remember how scared you were that the ice would crack under our feet? You clung to me for dear life, as if anything could happen.'

I gave a laugh but she didn't join in. Her expression betrayed nothing, it was as if she hadn't heard me, and perhaps she hadn't; only after I turned around and started walking again did I hear her voice behind me.

'That time we came boating here, Alica and I', she said, 'it was also summer, like now … the sun was beating down … And we stripped to our swimsuits …'

She spoke slowly and thoughtfully, as if talking to herself, but loudly enough for her words to reach me. I stopped again.

'I was rowing, Alica was sitting opposite me and dipped her hand in the water, probably to feel how cold it was, and suddenly a fish leapt out of the water, right by her hand. It had flung itself up into the air, really high, perhaps half a metre.'

All of a sudden, she gave a loud laugh. That's a sound I hadn't heard her make for a long time.

'The fright it gave her, dear old Alica! She got splashed and gave such a start that we nearly capsized', she said, laughing again, more loudly. 'But the fish wasn't going to hurt her, it just wanted to welcome her. To say hello to the silly girl.'

I remembered her laughter being different. Now it sounded deep and dry-throated, like a sweaty lumberjack, axe in hand, guffawing at a joke he had just heard. I glanced at her in surprise and was met by a mocking, triumphant gaze; I realised it was Agraphia looking at me.

'And what did it say to her?' I asked. 'I mean, what did the fish say to Alica?'

She stared at me for a moment wordlessly as if she were trying to read me and wanted to get to the last page before replying.

'What are you doing here?' she said eventually, but I wasn't sure if this was what the fish had said to Alica or what Agraphia was saying to me.

I tried, I really tried my utmost to love what remained of her. Or what she was about to become. Or what she might become. I wasn't being choosy, it's just that I couldn't work out what I was dealing with at any given moment. Love, in the sense we normally understand it, is neither here nor there in this context. It would be an unnecessary distraction.

2.t The soul! I can quite understand why Štefan has a problem with it, so it wasn't hard to promise I wouldn't use the word in his presence. To be honest, I also feel there is something about the word that rankles, something calculating, an attempt to stir the emotions. If you say the word 'soul' out loud, you will immediately sense that it emanates a kind of priestly, well-rehearsed kindliness. It is no accident that while the collocation a 'good soul' is quite common in Slovak, I have never heard of anyone being called an 'evil soul', and it is quite symptomatic that the word 'evildoer' doesn't include the word 'soul'. As if you would never automatically imagine that a soul might be nasty or malicious.

Štefan, who is a linguist, might say that this impression is, to a large extent, based on the fact that the Slovak for 'soul', *duša*, (pronounced '*dooshah*'), is feminine, and the soft sibilant 'š' between the two vowels must also play a part – it is the reason we subconsciously assume that the soul has a warm-hearted, maternal nature. Things might be different if the word contained bilabial consonants, plosives like 't' or 'p', harsh sound clusters such as 'fr', 'chr', 'čmr', 'br', 'dž', or the downright aggressive 'gr'. That might give us a more realistic idea of what the word stands for but even then Štefan wouldn't regard it as a scientific term.

For me, in spite of this reservation, the word 'soul' seems the most apposite term for that blurry, elusive little cloud and I have no intention of giving it up – after all, it has been used by many eminent psychiatrists, only they are aware that the soul consists of good and evil in equal measure and that the more light it contains the darker the shadow it casts.

But maybe the Zen Buddhists are right to claim that the division into good and evil is nothing but misguided dualism. We have two legs, but at the same time there is just one leg. All you need is a little patience and practice.

5.0 From the moment she sidled up to us at Štrbské pleso, Alica never left our side. She kept herself at the back but always close by, and every now and then darted over to us uninvited and stuck her nose into our conversation. She was the one who, in this little shop in Smokovec selling keepsakes and Modra pottery, had once bought a plaque in bronze or maybe brass as a souvenir, engraved with the words 'The High Tatras' with the relief of an edelweiss against the backdrop of the Kriváň mountain. Unlike us, Alica wore a red windcheater, green hunting knickerbockers and thick white, knee-high socks, and Agraphia teased her that if she grew a beard she would look like a member of the mountain rescue team. Alica, I had to admit, had the right gear for mountain hiking, no evening gowns or heels for her! When she joined us at the table at lunchtime, I learned that on the occasion she had been here with Agraphia, a piano player used to entertain the guests and Alica had remarked that the piano made a burbling sound; now wasn't that a nice way of putting it? This piqued my interest as it brought back memories of the time I was here with her and, in particular, of an afternoon tea when an elderly gentleman in a black suit and a bow tie did indeed tickle the ivories. However, it wasn't at the Park Hotel but at the Grand that we listened to Slovak tangos by Dušan Pálka and operetta numbers by Gejza Dusík, and to the best of my recollection no one made any remarks about the piano burbling – with the narrow-mindedness of youth we both turned up our noses at this kind of musical entertainment.

Suddenly, even after all these years, I could visualise every detail of the pianist's face, with his cauliflower nose and flowing white locks, but I still didn't have the slightest idea who Alica was. 'You don't know her, full stop.' The next time she imposed herself upon us I tried a trick. 'Oh, now I know', I said, 'she's the slim blonde who used to dance in the Lúčnica folk ensemble, right?' But it didn't work. 'A blonde, ha!' Agraphia exclaimed and kept shaking her head and smiling at how profoundly wrong I was. End of story.

On our last day I planned an outing to another tarn, Skalnaté pleso. Back when we were young we had hiked up the rocky path below the cable car and treated ourselves to a hearty lunch in the cable car station halfway up as we admired the view. This time we took the cable car up, had just a Coca-Cola because the taciturn Eugénia frowned at any mention of food, and then waited outside the station for a car that wasn't completely full of people coming down from the Lomnica peak. By then I had given up the mantra altogether but it was a clear day and the mountains looked majestic from close up, as if they existed in their very own time, in eternity. I tried to direct her attention to the beauty of the present moment as small clouds, dressed lightly in their underwear, darted about the sky. I pointed out the mountain peaks and she looked at them without a word and, it seemed to me, also without interest, until her gaze at last came to rest on a white patch in a gorge below the Lomnické saddle. 'What's that over there?'

'Oh, that's just some summer snow', I said, 'you know the kind of snow that's lingered on in a spot the sun can't reach because summer is only fleeting here.'

'Exactly!' she exclaimed joyfully and I could tell from her voice that this was Agraphia speaking. 'That's exactly what Alica said when we were here: fleeting snow she called it. Can you see how it sits there, perching on half its rear, ready to come tumbling down any moment? Cross my heart, she used the exact same words. Fleeting snow! That's it!'

So much for the High Tatras. I don't like them.

1.9 This is how I was suddenly robbed of a chunk of my past. It is hard to put into words how that feels – it is as if you were trying to lean against a wall and suddenly found it was no longer there. If Lienka had died physically, it would have left me free to recall everything, since the dead don't fight back, they are happy to be brought back to life and re-enact their role, but she was still around, visibly and tangibly, the same familiar person, even if no longer the same being, but she had backed out of a shared memory before my very eyes, completely and inexorably, as if she had never set foot in it. She had called off her appearance, cancelled it, and no matter how hard you try, you can't braid a single lock of hair, you need at least two. All of a sudden, I was standing in one of the vast rooms of my life, lonely and lost. Robbed.

This wasn't about me, of course, but still. You can tell yourself there is no point being angry with someone who has fainted and doesn't respond when you try resuscitation, yet the question does cross your mind whether they are holding their breath on purpose and having a laugh at your expense. I was confused. Alica! Where did she come from? Was it me, only assigned a different name and gender? Did she feel the need to reincarnate me in this way so that she could put up with me? To be honest, I didn't recognise myself in Alica and her stories didn't ring any bells either, I didn't fit into them. Or was it because Agraphia needed reinforcements and she manufactured an ally in the shape of Alica? Was this her way of showing me that, while she might still be dependent on me physically, she could manage without me mentally? Or did she pick Alica as her own pseudonym? I couldn't tell.

Or perhaps, I thought in the end, it was the wise, farsighted Eugénia trying to free me of the heavy burden – all that ballast of human opinions, ideas and qualities we lug around with us – to stop it from dragging me down into a deep snowdrift? So that I would face the avalanche with a mind pristine and empty, like that of a Zen Buddhist?

Thanks but no thanks, I already have Čimborazka to take care of that. That's the reason he came into this world.

4.k Štefan was aware of Lienka's problems but had no idea that she had now turned into Agraphia. And being the logically-minded person that he was, he would have dismissed Eugénia out of hand – in his view only the primitive Menominee can consider a lunatic a genius. He would probably have said that I heard the grass growing on Lienka's grave. However, as a distinguished scientist – not that anyone had actually read his book on bilabial consonants, but the mere fact that it was published in America was enough to cement his reputation – he knew many specialists in various areas and he was the one who suggested and helped arrange the visit to the neurologist. Who else was I to turn to with the problem named Alica?

'To me it's obvious', said Štefan. 'It's her indirect way of crying for help. She uses Alica to send you an S.O.S., like the telegraph operator on the Titanic. Save our souls.'

'Please note that it was you who used the s-word, not me.'

'I just unpacked the English acronym for you', Štefan said. 'Stop playing with words.'

'Isn't it interesting', I said, 'when a ship is sinking, people demand that their souls be saved even though what they obviously want is for their bodies to be saved. They probably think that God is more likely to have mercy on their souls and that the bodies will somehow be able to jump on the bandwagon.'

'Stop playing with words', Štefan repeated, 'this is not the right time. Try to think what you can do to save her instead.'

'It's not like I haven't been trying', I said. 'Is it my fault that it's not working? Doctors are best equipped to save the body but, in this case, they too are out of their depth. The organic process in the brain is apparently like an avalanche, once it's set in motion it can't be stopped. And as for the soul, that's something your English sailors have known for a long time, a soul can't be rescued, it can only be saved. But I don't dare to play the saviour. At most, I can pray to the Saviour.'

'The Redeemer, in case you're interested', said Štefan. 'That's what the English call the Saviour. As far as I know the Menominee don't have a similar character or concept.'

And look where that has got them.

5.p Very soon the only one left was Eugénia in her inaccessible world. Sometimes, when she peered into the world we used to share, as if to make sure she wasn't missing anything in case it had changed in the meantime, it would result in some kind of calamity and Eugénia would retreat back into safety, frightened. There was no way back.

One day she decided to do the washing up, and when she left the kitchen she didn't turn the tap off, the water overflowed the blocked sink and flooded our neighbours. They rang our bell but to no avail, the ringing didn't penetrate Eugénia's world, or maybe she had decided not to let any strangers in. They had to wait for me to come back from the shops. On another occasion she was making coffee and left a small pan of water on the gas cooker until it started smouldering and the smoke reached the living room where I was browsing through a booklet on Slovak place names. Then there was the time she tried to clean a stain on the sofa using paint solvent and burnt through the upholstery. Once when I wasn't looking, she mistook petrol for vinegar and poured some into the bean soup I was making – the explosion singed her eyebrows and eyelashes and set the curtain on fire. It became dangerous to leave her alone even for a moment as I had no idea when and why she might try to emerge from her apathy.

It is challenging to live like this and you can't do it for any length of time, no matter how hard you try to fool yourself. The critical moment came one autumn afternoon. Eugénia was sleeping on the pull-out couch in the living room because that is where the TV set was – I don't know if she was really aware of what was happening on the screen, probably not, since she never changed channels, but the flickering screen and the hum must have had a calming effect on her. Sometimes she would startle me with an incomprehensible shout that I could hear through the door I had left slightly ajar, and when I peered inside I would find her smiling, imitating the characteristic sound of some animal on the set: she would repeat a cockerel's crow, a pig's oink or she would bleat along with a sheep. She seemed to get on fine with animals, their voices had the ability to rouse her from her daydreams. Better than human voices, it seemed. Certainly better than my voice.

Eugénia would sleep irregularly, at odd times, regardless of the time of day; maybe inside an avalanche eternal gloom prevails and you can't tell the time when you are within it. I had to be constantly on my guard on the other side of the slightly open door. Sleep would come upon me in short bursts, sometimes even while I was standing up in the kitchen, but on that morning, worn down by exhaustion, I was fast asleep in bed and only woke up when I was shaken by our next-door neighbour, Mrs Frátriková.

'Your door was open', she said, 'so I came in. In case you're looking for your wife, she's at our place, you can come and get her.'

It turned out that Eugénia had woken up and when she couldn't find me in the flat – apparently she didn't check the bedroom, or if she did, failed to spot me huddled under the blankets – she panicked and ran out into the rain as she was, in her nightdress and slippers. Our neighbour found her on the pavement, frightened and confused. 'There's nobody at home', was all she said in answer to Mrs Frátriková's questions. 'Nobody at all. Nobody anywhere', and burst into tears.

When I came to collect her, she got up from a chair in the hall and met me halfway without saying a word, but as well as anxiety

I saw something resembling relief in her eyes. Recognition, maybe. I took her by the hand and she smiled.

'It's just a minor misunderstanding', I said to Mr and Mrs Frátrik at the door. 'She had just woken up and in that woozy state she thought I had left, so she went out to look for me. Thank you for taking care of her, it was very kind of you.'

Later, I wondered about that look in her eyes when she saw me, and who it was that she had recognised in me. Who she took me for. A husband was a category from a completely different world, a word for ticking a box on a form – after all, I no longer thought of her as a wife, formal titles and social conventions having long ceased to play any role in our lives. All that was left was two people riding together in a lift packed so tight they could feel each other's breath, and that journey was taking a long time. Judging by the look in her eyes, I was someone close, at least provisionally so, a stop-gap measure: since the person she loved wasn't around, she loved the one who was. Maybe she saw me as a kind of liaison officer, a connection with the world she had left. Or an interpreter, perhaps? I don't know. She was pleased to see me, so maybe she really did love me now, although probably not as much as the animals on TV. They were able to cheer her up while I couldn't. But then I remembered the look in her eyes, the very first look as she was sitting on the chair in the Frátriks' hallway, full of almost animal anxiety, as if she were no longer a being, just a creature … as it turned out, all I could do was give her a fright.

I failed because I had let it happen, and it makes no difference that I had done so unwittingly, by mistake. It was like stomach cramps, an unbearable feeling, and with the best will in the world I couldn't guarantee that it wouldn't happen again. I swore I would not, must not, let it happen again.

A week later, with Štefan's assistance, Eugénia was admitted to hospital.

4.1 Mississauga, Cheektowaga, Madawaska, Kalamazoo. Still here. Waukegan, Kankakee. Fossils. Petawawa, Maniwaki. Gidra, Tuhrina, Bruty, Lutiha, Chlm, Ptrukša. Still here. And so are Ohek, Jovsa, Koromľa, Zbudza.

I am still here, alone in the empty flat, empty and with a load of empty time. Now that the flat and I have become so similar, it wasn't difficult for us to find a way of cohabiting. We weren't curious about one another, didn't need to talk, the flat knew how to rebuke me silently and I knew how to ignore it without saying anything. But I had no idea what to do with these unexpected riches, a full twenty-four hours a day.

After I basically slept through the first forty-eight hours, time bared its toothless pink gums at me, making me flee from the flat. Into emptiness. That's where I met Ed with his Buddha in pill form, for quick use, and it did help at first. Although the Buddha is stocky and fills a lot of empty space, nobody was as good at filling space as Štefan. He didn't make me sit cross-legged or empty my mind, and the encyclopaedia of women's buttocks that he had given me as a present was always there, ready to browse for hours, over and over again, whenever I felt a sudden urge to admire dead butterflies pinned down by a camera lens. But what mattered most was that with Štefan there was always something to talk about, I could take that for granted. All I had to do was raise a subject and he would immediately pounce on it like a Greco-Roman wrestler, performing a double nelson of elementary logic and scientific perspective. After a conversation with him I would always feel I was coming out of a school lesson, overwhelmed by the sheer amount of unnecessary new information.

A brief summary of the key points of Štefan's research project had recently been published in the linguistics journal of the Academy of Sciences; the paper was supposed to increase his chances of getting a grant. I'm not sure he succeeded because the very next issue of the journal carried a polemic piece by Professor Ondraško challenging some of Štefan's premises. The professor claimed that the most expressive consonant clusters – *dz, dž, fr, brm, pt* or *gr* – were precisely the ones that had entered Old Church Slavonic either from the languages of the tribes that had originally settled in what is now Slovakia or those with whom the Slavs had maintained trade, cultural or military relations after arriving in the area. Despite the sober scientific language one could feel that the professor regarded these cuckoo eggs in the same way as the exotic illnesses with which the Spanish conquistadors had infected the innocent, healthy native Americans.

I'm just a layman, of course, but I found the principal idea fascinating. If the white immigrants from the Old World could adopt the native Indian place names, why would the Slavs not have done the same? After all, according to the most probable hypothesis the names of the rivers Hron and Váh are of Germanic-Quadi origin, and the Celts and Dacians must also have left some fossils behind.

'Take Oľza, for example', I said to Štefan. 'Sirk. Gortva. They are all still here. I could go on. Bruty, Chropov, Zbudza. Aren't these the remnants of the Celts, the Marcomanni and the Quadi, before they were all swallowed by the avalanche? Just go through the list of Slovak place names if you don't believe me, it's full of fossils like these.'

'That's irrelevant from the point of view of my research', Štefan replied. 'I don't study place names, only notional words in the Slovak language, their phonetic aspect in particular. The expressive wealth of the Slovak language, if you will, or rather, the advanced onomatopoeia of the Slovak ethnic group. I'm not interested in the origin of sounds and words, that I leave to etymologists. My esteemed colleague Ondraško is a lousy shot, instead of the target he shoots around corners, but if I thought it worth responding, I would say that the fact that the Slovaks have adopted these kinds of sound clusters with the aim of expressing more clearly a moral or emotional attitude only demonstrates their creative approach to language. The professor should be careful, I know very well which way the wind is blowing, the good professor is trying to rehash the old fairy tale of the peace-loving, dove-like nature of our people, in the guise of linguistics. As if the more expressive elements had been imposed on our soft, mellifluous Slovak tongue by foreigners, especially the ancient Teutons and, later, the German colonists who moved here following repeated invitations from the Hungarian kings.'

'Like Baumgartner from Banská Bystrica, for example', I said. 'But wouldn't it be nice if the Slovaks had also left similar relics behind? I mean some unmistakably, purely Slovak fossils that someone will dig out from under the snow sometime in future, after we've been buried by the avalanche. Place names like Drienčie or Bôrka. Hlivištia, Čertižné, Imeľ, Bachureň, Drábsko. But the most wonderful place name, to my mind, is Braväcovo, with that 'ä' in the middle. That is the absolute quintessence of Slovakness, one that would make us clearly recognisable even in a mound of snow.'

'I'm beginning to wish that your avalanche came tumbling down', said Štefan, 'just to shut you up.'

'It's coming, it's coming, don't you worry', I said. 'Maybe it's already on its way, quietly, steadily, and as we know, once an avalanche has been set in motion it can't be stopped. But have no fear, humankind will survive, although a new species of snow people might emerge, people who will have learned to shovel snow so that they can scramble out from under an avalanche, or at least punch a comfortable hole in the snow to breathe through. I think this will represent a turning point in human development similar to the one when an ape climbed down from the tree and stood upright on its two hind legs for the first time. Those with more foresight, who don't want to be caught unawares, have already started to practise digging, haven't you noticed? The only problem is, when you're inside an avalanche it's hard to tell which way is up and which is down so there's a danger that many people will dig themselves deeper in the hole by mistake.'

But Štefan has no sense of humour and was obviously bored by my avalanche jokes. He kept drumming his fingers on the table till I was done with my speech and then said, as if he hadn't heard my final words at all:

'I have to disappoint you: '*ä*' isn't quite as unique a sound as you seem to think, the Germans and the Finns also have it, not to mention the Slovenes, they have five different ways of pronouncing the vowel '*e*'. If I were you I wouldn't pin too many hopes on '*ä*', it's a sound condemned to extinction. These days it is being pronounced in a distinct way only in two or three villages and with the passage of time, as the sound becomes obsolete, the letter denoting it will also be eliminated. There won't be anything left to dig out of that avalanche of yours.'

Obviously, he always has to have the last word.

2.u Seeing her off from the platform was easier said than done, but how was I to guess when her train was leaving? I could have asked a railway worker familiar with the timetable, the neurologist or the psychiatrist, but even they wouldn't have been able to tell me which train Eugénia might want to catch – would she take an intercity or would she be content with a stopping train? Or when she would pack her evening gown, frilly blouse and heels, and set out for the station by herself, on foot …

During this empty time, farewell words would stampede through my head willy-nilly like a herd of wild horses. Runaway horses. 'Whatever I've done,' I would say to her in my head, 'whatever we may have felt about each other … looking back on it now, in hindsight … only now do I really see you … do I really see what you mean to me ... you are still whole, a complete being to me ... still, always ...'

Or something along those lines. Stammering, I would sink my teeth into a word only to spit out the counterfeit coin straight away. 'You are precious,' I wanted to say to her, 'not only to me, not because of me nor because you are a woman ... but in and of yourself, as a human being, the bearer of a unique soul ...'

And more nonsense of that kind. 'I know,' I told myself, 'Alica's hostility wasn't aimed at me, she wasn't my enemy, you only summoned her to your aid, to your rescue ... to help you retain your dignity in this unbearable world of ours. Please forgive me for not understanding that, for pressing your nose, like a kitten's, into the bowl of our past as if what mattered was our common past ... as if you didn't really exist outside of it, independently of it ...'

I remembered that she once said, it was just a throwaway remark, that I had never said 'I love you' to her. But then again, she hadn't exactly lavished declarations of love on me either, that was something we had in common. That is why we were close. 'As for love' – as I tried to explain in the hustle and bustle on the platform, amidst the roaring of the electric engine and the banging of closing doors – 'as for that white-hot emotion between two people, I'd rather not talk about it. It may exist, it does happen, but that's not what this is about. It would just get in the way. I love you because we're both here only fleetingly, and I am grateful that you allowed me to watch from a distance as you went your way. Forgive me if I didn't always do it with the requisite attention, if I let myself be distracted by other things.'

I couldn't do it. Who would be interested in this kind of drivel that sounded almost as if it wasn't coming out of my mouth, while standing on a platform, with the train about to depart? Who would have the patience to hear me out as I fumbled for words? And even if I had managed to find the right words, it was too late, she had already taken her seat in the compartment – it was a window seat so I could still see her but she could no longer hear me. The guard blew his whistle and the train moved off. All I could do was wave and stand there for a while, my eyes on the last carriage, filled with that sweetly stinging, knotty pain typical of love on the platform.

Here's the thing: the reason why the word love is so popular is that everyone can make it mean whatever they like.

5·9 I might still have seen her sitting there but I could no longer see inside her.

The first time I came to visit and she saw me at the door, she stared at me for a moment in silence before blurting out suddenly: 'Are we going home?' Then she pulled out the drawer of her bedside table and started rummaging in it feverishly. She took out a hairbrush, a wristwatch, a box of tic-tacs, a roll of toilet paper …

I failed yet again, I didn't take her home. Perhaps she initially took me for an emissary, a messenger of the flat she was missing, but once she realised that this wasn't who I was, she lost interest in me. She sat down on the side of her bed in her dressing gown and started hurling things back into the drawer, higgledy-piggledy: the table was made of metal and the drawer made a noise every time an object was dropped in. She picked up the box with the little white sweets, shook one out absent-mindedly and put it in her mouth. As she sucked on it her cheeks sank in like those of an old woman who had forgotten to put in her dentures. Dr Gebauer, the psychiatrist, explained that in addition to her primary illness she had now become depressed and that it was hard to tell what part the two conditions played in bringing about her present state of mind. However, depression could be treated, or at least suppressed, by medication. That was their primary goal at the moment and if I was able to contribute to this in any way …

That is how my next desperate idea was born. When you have too much time on your hands you latch on to any nonsense just to rid yourself of that burden. I imagined that I could bring Katinka D. to visit her and that this person to whom she had once been close would remind Eugénia of the good old days and tempt her back into our world. Basically, I wanted to use Katinka as bait. Because I obviously lacked the power to be that myself. I was no longer attractive.

And so, one morning I caught a trolleybus. It was a long way, I had plenty of time to think, but that doesn't mean that my thoughts made sense. I don't know what I had been thinking – that the institution wouldn't mind entrusting a student or inmate to a complete stranger who didn't even know her surname? Yes, that was what I thought. I was convinced that Lienka's colleagues would remember her and would be happy to help, that after all that time Katinka D. would also remember her with a childlike devotion and that she would be happy to go and see her with her husband, whom she surely still remembered. I could have been her father, after all, couldn't I? Or foster father, at least.

I saw her in my mind's eye as she had once been, as if there was no trapdoor, no black hole of history. 'Remember how sorry you were for the mole who was so hot in his fur coat?' I will say to her and in this way, amid cheerful chatter, we would arrive at the hospital. Seeing her, Eugénia would clap her hands, Lienka would leap out of her belly and soon she and Katinka would be hugging each other, maybe even shedding a few tears together – Lienka had never been disposed to cry but children's crying is contagious. Sounds absurd? Of course it does, but all sorts of things do happen and sometimes I was just as wide of the mark as Eugénia.

The matter was speedily resolved in the corridor. After I finally managed to explain who Katinka was to a former colleague of Lienka's who had come to the door, she shook her head.

'She's no longer with us', she said.

'I see', I replied. 'Any idea where I might find her?'

She gave me a strange look. The kind Agraphia sometimes treated me to.

'In the nether world', she said, 'if she is anywhere. Down's syndrome children don't live long, most of them die before they reach thirty.'

She walked me to the door and before locking up she shouted after me: 'And remember me to Magdika. Tell her Žela sends her love, I'm sure she'll remember me.'

Sure, I thought. She no longer remembers her own name but she has definitely not forgotten Žela.

I really don't know what I had imagined. Not this. On my way home, my head now clear, I comforted myself that perhaps it was better this way. Who knows, maybe instead of happy memories Katinka would have stirred up Eugénia's grief over an unfulfilled dream, the fact that she was forced to swap a child for a dog. No, I couldn't see into Eugénia, but at that point I realised that, in fact, I had never seen into Lienka either; I saw only what she had chosen to show me. Now that I thought of it, we had been sending each other postcards from our respective inner worlds – of sunsets, waves breaking on the beach, Gothic cathedrals, ruins of old castles … As usual with postcards, they showed everything in colour and looking more beautiful and radiant than in reality, as if wanting to display it larger than life.

When I tried to discuss this with Štefan he stopped me after my first words.

'I won't listen to this', his said. 'This verbal swagger of yours. Instead of trying to get the old girl out of the lurch you're treating her illness like an allotment where you can cultivate your own intellectual life.'

I know that Štefan is not keen on such abstract, unscientific reflections, for him they are pure phantasmagorias. But I have noticed that lately he has been referring to her as 'the old girl'. I don't think it's because he has trouble switching between Magdaléna, Lienka, Agrafia or Eugénia, he doesn't even know about the last two names; it is something he has simply picked up from me. He must have thought that you have to tiptoe around someone who is sick, or maybe he didn't want to offend me, as the next of kin, and 'the old girl' was an easy way out of an awkward situation.

For me she will forever remain a girl because when a boy and a girl grow old together they can never grow old in one another's eyes.

1.r, 2.v, 3.h, 4.m, 5.r

It is rude to eavesdrop on other people's conversations but the young man on the trolleybus was so loud that it was unavoidable.

'Listen, Sweetiepie, you've got to believe me', his voice boomed through the quiet carriage, 'it's all nonsense, I've never cheated on you. You know it's true. Are you listening to me? I would never cheat on you, darling, 'cause I love you, I swear to God, you've got to believe me. And I hope you'll be faithful to me, too. What? Of course I believe you, Sweetiepie, but you've got to believe me too.'

I tried to work out who he was talking to: in the seat in front of him there sat an older woman in a headscarf, with her back to him, and behind was a chap wearing glasses and a bandage on his wrist but the young man kept looking down, into his lap. Then I noticed his left arm resting on the window pane. He was talking to his phone. I'm not saying it was quite an avalanche, but in his shouting the quiet hiss of snow sliding down the slope was clearly audible.

'Did you know that apart from their sense of smell hedgehogs also have an extremely well-developed sense of hearing?' I asked

Štefan. 'Apparently, they can hear a caterpillar munching leaves from ten metres away.'

'That may well be', Štefan replied noncommittally.

'Seeing as you're a scientist, maybe you can tell me how that was discovered. I don't imagine they could ask the hedgehog.'

'Easy', he said. 'They discovered it by experimenting. Presumably, hedgehogs feed on caterpillars, otherwise it wouldn't work. So, they would just take a caterpillar and some leaves and gradually move them further and further away from the hedgehog – first one metre, then two and so on, until the hedgehog let the caterpillar munch in peace. The good old method of trial and error.'

'I remember we once had a hedgehog in our house', I said, 'when I was young. My mother found it in the cemetery. It spent the whole day kipping behind the kitchen stove and only crawled out at night and would go stomping around the flat. If I had thought of it back then, and if I had found a caterpillar and some leaves, I could have carried out the experiment myself.'

'You didn't think of it because you lack a scientific approach to the world', Štefan said, 'that's your main problem. 'You don't have a scientific way of thinking.'

'Forget about hedgehogs' hearing', I said. 'What really interests me today is whether I should regard hedgehogs as creatures or beings?'

'There you go again!' Štefan exclaimed.

A middle-aged couple sitting at the next table turned to look at him so I decided not to take this debate any further. In fact, I was quite clear on the subject. I believe that hedgehogs are beings. I remember that ours used to smack its lips loudly when it ate, just like human beings.

'Shut your trap', a woman said to an unshaven fellow standing in front of her with a plastic bottle in his hand, the kind that mineral water usually comes in. He was wearing a blue shell suit jacket and a pair of mottled camouflage trousers and didn't look like the kind of person who would be spending money on mineral water.

'Take it while it's going!' The man gave a laugh and took a swig from the bottle. 'It might be your last chance to get yourself a well-heeled boyfriend.'

'Shut your trap', the woman said again. Another homeless man was sitting next to her on the bench in a heavy woollen coat that must once have been quite smart. His matted hair was so thick it looked like he was wearing a fur hat; he was raking his fingers through it and each time he found a louse he crushed it on his knee with a fingernail.

The woman stood up, 'Let's go over there', she said, indicating another bench with her head, 'we can talk in peace there. Without any drunken talk.' Close to, her face was rough, as if carved out of wood and impregnated with a coating against the weather. It resembled an Indian totem head.

'I once read somewhere that Shakespeare used twenty thousand words in his plays', I said to Štefan. 'Or maybe thirty thousand, I forget. Some English linguist has counted them. Unfortunately, I don't know exactly how many words there are in Slovak.'

'The old Dictionary of the Slovak Language, the one published in the nineteen-fifties, contained over a hundred thousand', Štefan said. 'And that presumably doesn't include many of the words in use now.'

'Goodness!' I said 'A hundred thousand! Incredible. What are we to do with this huge mass of words? What use can we make of it? I think the average Slovak doesn't use more than a thousand words, that's more than plenty for him.'

'Don't exaggerate', Štefan said. 'If you just consider all those people with a degree who use technical terminology, you get ...'

'But I'm talking about Slovak words, not terms borrowed from other languages', I said. 'If we examined what an average Slovak says in a day, I mean all his utterances, we might be in for a surprise. I think we would find that many get along with just five hundred basic expressions.'

'Don't exaggerate', Štefan repeated.

'Just admit it, when was the last time you personally heard someone use the word *bľosa*?' I said. 'Or *čmrlákať sa*? Go on, tell the truth!'

'I don't know', he said. 'I can't remember. And it doesn't matter because if I haven't heard them, I'm sure Irenka will have heard someone use them.'

'She had to trudge through remote hamlets and shepherds' huts to find them', I said, 'and what for? A thousand words, that's quite enough for a Slovak. And do you know why he never dips into the remaining ninety-nine thousand? Because he doesn't have any thoughts in his head to make that necessary. That's the real tragedy. That's something no linguist can figure out.'

'So what's all this about?' the woman asked. 'What do you want me to do?' She didn't sit down, we were both standing there beside the bench.

'Nothing', I said. 'As I said, what I'm wondering is, would you like to spend a night under a roof again, just for a change. Somewhere warm, in my flat. And if you felt like it, you could also have a bath while you're there, wash your hair, wash some of your clothes, and so on.'

The woman looked me up and down openly and unashamedly.

'I'm not that kind of person, if that's what you think', she said in the end.

'Neither am I', I said. 'I just thought you might like a little bit of comfort, that's all.'

She kept staring at me as if she were short-sighted and couldn't see my face properly. She wore an old pair of jeans and a red windcheater with a greasy stain on the sleeve.

'I might have some women's clothes at home as well', I said. 'If you can use them, you could take some.'

'Has your wife died?' she asked. 'Or has she left you?' As she laughed, I saw that several of her upper teeth were missing. 'She's left you for someone else?'

The gaps lent her smile a vampire-like quality. It looked malevolent to me. I shook my head.

'Let's just say she left', I said.

'I hope she doesn't end up like me', said the woman, looking serious now. 'You probably can't tell but I've got a diploma from nursing college, I worked as a hospital nurse for years. In a geriatric clinic. It's hard work. All those old people and you're expected to fuss over them all the time, feed them, carry bedpans, some patients even need their nappies changed... I've done my share of honest work, don't get the wrong idea.'

She said this proudly, almost provocatively, as if she saw doubt in my face and wanted to stifle it in advance.

'Don't get me wrong, old people are also human beings, many of them used to be clever, some were quite high up... like we had this famous actor in the clinic, I'm not going to give his name away... but when they keep bossing you about even though they don't really know what they want, when you have to keep reminding yourself you're supposed to be nice to them, it gets you down after a while. It's hard to like them, not every-one is up to it, you start taking pills to cope, if you can get hold of them, you might have a drink or two to steady yourself, and then, if on top of it all, you meet the wrong man...'

It's not that she smelled really bad from close to, but every now and then a whiff of something dank and earthy wafted from her as from a damp haystack. A decent beautician and hairdresser might have been able revive a hint of her faded former beauty, but I just couldn't picture her in a nurse's uni-form. The story of the down-and-out from Trenčín or Karlova Ves sounded more amusing to me. More plausible.

'But I still don't understand, do you work for some charity or what?' she asked suddenly. 'Or do you just want to do a good deed?' She gave me that gap-toothed grin again. 'To wipe a sin from the record?'

'How long are you gonna let this guy chat you up, Zdena?' the man from the other bench shouted, raising the bottle in his hand. 'Get a move on or there'll be nothing left for you!' Maybe he said not Zdena but Dana, it was hard to make out from where I was standing.

She looked in his direction. 'What the hell is he banging on about?' she muttered and turned back to face me. 'Let me ask you something: can I bring my pals? Never mind the way they look, like that one over there, he's got a degree, he's an engineer…'

'My sins aren't quite so grave', I said. I was beginning to sober up. 'And my flat isn't really big enough for all of you.'

'Then let's just forget about it', she said. 'It's not that cold yet, I've got somewhere to sleep and it's more fun here with them.'

She fixed her eyes on me, examining me without sympathy, with dry eyes.

'I'm doing all right as I am', she said eventually. 'I'm not short of anything. You'd be surprised how many things one can manage without, and how easy it is. If I wanted to, I could take a shower at the shelter for a few cents, they'd also give me some clothes, so that's the least of my problems. To be honest, I wouldn't want to go back, not in a month of Sundays, I wouldn't want to be lumbered with all those stupid worries again … But if you want to do a good deed, give us ten euros, we'll make good use of it.'

'I'm glad you're enjoying your meal', I said to Štefan. 'You're smacking your lips as loudly as that hedgehog of mine.'

By this time, we were sitting in Harmónia, our third restaurant of the day, and I was ordering a starter of goose liver with prunes and cranberries.

'And one more thing about hedgehogs. You know I mentioned that their hearing is better than ours. I believe that in the past, when the Menominee still lived by hunting, their hearing was also nearly as good. I don't claim they could hear caterpillars munching leaves but I'm sure they could tell from as far as a hundred metres away if it was an opossum crunching beetles or a wild hog gnawing on roots. These days they can tell from a kilometre if it's a Kawasaki or a Harley Davidson roaring through the forest. Maybe they can even tell by the sound whose motorbike it is, but that would be a different matter.'

'This is my last stop', Štefan said. 'I'm not prepared to keep up with you any longer. In case you don't know, gluttony is one of the seven deadly sins. Do you have a hole in your stomach or what? I can hardly breathe after that knuckle of pork at the City Brewery.'

I wish it was just a hole in the stomach; I felt so riddled with holes that I could feel the wind blowing through me. Through and through. I had to do something to plug those holes.

'And I bet', I said, 'that a Menominee shaman could hear from one end of the reservation to the other how your soul, pardon the expression, endlessly chews over the bilabial consonants of a language that is on the verge of extinction. Maybe he could rid you of this bad habit, except that you've never set foot in a reservation.'

'If I were you, I wouldn't overestimate the reservation Indians', Štefan said. 'They spend their time sitting around on a bench with a bottle in a brown paper bag, getting wasted. If you asked them they wouldn't know their own name.'

'I don't have a tenner but I can give you a fiver', I said. 'That will be enough to buy some cider, for your friends as well. And please forgive me for bothering you. Sometimes I have crazy ideas, but I meant well.'

She took a good look at the five euro note, folded it in half and put it in her windcheater pocket.

'Why should I be angry', she said, patting her pocket with her hand twice as if to double-check the note was there. 'It's just that you meet all sorts of people these days, some think they can be horrible to folks like us, like we're mangy or something. I don't mean you, but you have to be careful.'

'Excuse me for a moment', I said to Štefan. The toilets were in the middle of a corridor between two rooms of the restaurant, the men's toilet had a basin with a mirror, and a urinal as well as a cubicle. I headed for the cubicle and once there, stuck a finger down my throat.

'What's wrong?' Štefan asked when I came back. He must have thought I'd been away a long time. 'Is something the matter?'

'Not really', I replied. 'I'm just pissed off that I haven't managed to return a fur coat to its owner. I was too late.'

'What kind of fur coat, what are you talking about?' he asked in surprise.

'A fur coat', I said. 'Made of moleskin. A rare, valuable specimen, but it's not about the price. What bothers me is that I've failed again. By the time I was ready to act it was too late.'

'Don't expect me to solve your riddles on a stomach that's this stuffed', said Štefan. 'Pay up and let's get out of here.'

The tables and chairs in front of the café across the street had already been put away but it was a nice autumn day, rich in colour. It reminded me of the time, two or three years back, when Lienka and I were sitting here enjoying a cup of coffee and a cream slice. It was summer, the rays of the sun were licking us agreeably; a group of passing Japanese tourists stopped on the corner to take pictures of a street that was shabby in a picturesque kind of way. I luxuriated in the idyll, pleased that I didn't have to trudge around a strange city with a herd of other people, as I listened not even with half but only a quarter of an ear to Lienka, who was talking. The strange thing is: I remember the cream slice we had but have only the vaguest recollection of what she was talking about. I think she was discussing a problem to do with some second job, I'm not even sure if it concerned her or a colleague – I guess the question was whether to take it or not. I can't remember the conclusion she reached, I didn't consider it important at the time. I told myself that for Lienka an integral part of an idyll is to talk, while for me it isn't about trying to work out the meaning of her words, just quietly drinking in the sound of her voice. I liked its melody.

'Hang on a minute', I said to Štefan as we were walking up Michalská Street. 'I've heard that there's a restaurant in this courtyard where they do a excellent onion soup served in a bread bowl. Let me invite you to sample this speciality, you can't overeat on soup.'

'No way', he said, 'not a chance in hell. I've had it with food. I'd better say goodbye right here, I've got Irenka waiting for me in the office anyway.'

'Give her my love', I said. 'Tell her to wear those tight trousers, they really show off her bum.'

He waved his hand dismissively without turning back. Or maybe he made a cross over me. As I watched him walk away I thought I detected a slight hunching of his back. This is how my step-me was taking his leave; resolutely and without turning back. My monozygotic twin.

'If a hedgehog is a being with a soul, you must have a soul, too,' I thought. 'There's nothing you can do about that. It's no use running away, one day it will catch up with you and reveal itself in its full glory. And then with all your exact science and objective approach to the world you'll be screwed.'

I set off as well, not for the restaurant and the soup, just running on empty. Into the emptiness. Under St Michael's Gate a small gaggle of tourists huddled round the brass disc set into the pavement and showing directions and distances to world cities. They were probably Americans because their guide asked in English: 'Anyone here from New York?' and an elderly man in grey-black checked trousers raised his hand. 'This plaque here tells you how far from home you are', said the guide, pointing to the ground.

I had never done it before, so I decided to take a look as well. The distance between St Michael's Gate and New York was 6,856 kilometres, Beijing was 7,433 kilometres away, but the city furthest away, 15,914 kilometres, was Sydney. Madrid was 1,865 kilometres away, Paris 1,094, Rome 783 and Vienna could manage only a measly 57 kilometres. San Francisco or New Orleans were not included because they are not world cities. And Petawawa was clearly so unimportant (or so near) that the plaque didn't deem it worthy of being mentioned.

Here's the thing: the door to the ward was locked, I had to ring the bell. Instead of a nurse, a young doctor opened the door. He recognised me and let me in straight away.

'The good news', he said as we walked down the corridor, 'is that we've got the depression more or less under control, but as for the primary illness, unfortunately, the prognosis is poor. I must warn you that there has been a further decline. But please don't let that show on your face.'

He stopped outside the doctors' room. 'Just a moment, let me get you a white coat so that we don't upset the patients unnecessarily', he said. The white coat was too big for me, my arms were lost in its long sleeves. It made me feel like an angel with broken wings.

The corridors in the old building were very high and wide enough for a few small tables and benches. The doctor left me standing by a bench and went in. He was gone for a while, then the door opened and Eugénia appeared. She was standing there stock-still, as if searching her mind for a reason to move further and failing to find one. She was unkempt and wore a blue hospital dressing gown, carelessly tied, from which a night dress peeked out, but to me she seemed beautiful, in that slightly bitter and singular way everything appears to be when we think we are seeing it for the last time.

The doctor gave her a gentle push from behind. 'Look who's here to see you', he said in a sonorous, cheerful voice.

Her eyes reluctantly tore themselves away from something only she could see. They jumped over to me, then to the tall window behind me and back again; I could see that she was desperately casting around for some memories of the customs of the world she had decided to abandon. Eventually she smiled and took a step towards me.

'Pleased to meet you, doctor', she said. The smile that clung to her face like a man hanging by his fingernails from a ninth-floor window made me want to weep, but the doctor was standing next to me and I remembered his warning.

'My name is Čimborazka', I said and shook her by the hand.

INTERVIEW WITH THE AUTHOR

In September 2016 Pavel Vilikovský talked about *Fleeting Snow* to Jana Németh in the Slovak daily *Denník N*.

In 2014 you won the Anasoft Litera Prize for your book First and Last Love. *You said that its title was somewhat misleading, and that you ended up having to explain what you meant by love. It seems to me that the title* Fleeting Snow *is no less misleading. How did you come up with it?*

It's something of a makeshift title. I came up with it while I was working on the book. It didn't occur to me until I was writing a scene set in the Tatras, in which a patch of snow remains visible. I thought a conversation about it would reinforce the image of an avalanche, which for me is pivotal to the story. Basically, the book is just a kind of loose rambling on about a variety of themes, but the avalanche is – as the saying goes – the red thread running through it. The avalanche of individual but also collective or social, forgetfulness and loss of memory.

And maybe also the loss of the soul?

That raises the question of which part of the soul is constituted by memory. I think it is a substantial part because consciousness, which the narrator of my book calls the soul, is something we piece together out of our experiences. And as we start to lose them or forget them, the soul also becomes increasingly impoverished.

Čimborazka says that once an avalanche is triggered it can no longer be stopped. But can you dig yourself out of it?

There have been cases proving that it's possible. But the fact that it can't be stopped is something I found in an encyclopaedia; I've never been buried under an avalanche myself. But it helped me create this parallel with illness – the loss of memory – which, once it starts, can't be stopped. However, I would like to ask potential readers to take what's written here with a pinch of salt. Rather than some profound wisdom, it's just meant to nudge them to think for themselves about the issues raised in the book.

The book contains quite a few serious issues, dealing as it does with memory loss, impending death, the meaning of life, as well as God, but it's all written with a very light touch, in an almost jolly tone. Was that your intention?

I wanted the book to be amusing. That's what I was trying to achieve and it's what made me write the book in the first place. Shortly before I started on it I had finished a book about a fairly repugnant character, *The Story of an Ordinary Man* and I needed to cleanse my head and my lungs, relax by doing something amusing. I'm not saying it's amusing the whole time but I tried to put on a cheerful face.

Čimborazka also puts on a cheerful face, particularly at the beginning, endearing himself to the reader by talking about love and the soul, but his views are constantly juxtaposed with those of Štefan Kováč, his 'step-twin', who takes a much more pragmatic approach to things. How did you come up with the name Čimborazka, and whose views are closer to your own?

The word 'Čimborazka' just popped into my head one day. It had this cheerfully nonsensical ring to it, and I made a note of it. In this book, Čimborazka longs to be carefree, but that's not really allowed these days. As for Kováč – I don't know how he wormed his way into it. I don't even know if he's just another version of Čimborazka or a different person altogether. The fact is, when I look at my previous works, I prefer the parts which contain dialogue, and I rarely have more than two characters. I find having them discuss things preferable to just narrating what interests me. Mind you, this is not something I do consciously. Only in hindsight, when a character additional to the narrator starts hanging around the book do I realise that I've done it again. Although these two men – Čimborazka and Kováč – hold opposing views and positions, both are legitimate. Čimborazka is prone to banging on about the soul and raising spiritual themes, which I abhor profoundly. But there are moments when I succumb to them myself, despite my profound abhorrence.

At one stage Čimborazka tells Kováč that he can hear the avalanche coming tumbling down. When you look at what's happening around us today, doesn't it seem to you that the avalanche has hit us already?

No, I don't think we've been buried yet. But I would say that I can already hear the rumbling of the snow. However, when I recall my childhood and how we used to live then, and compare it with the present day, I have the feeling that it's been rumbling for an awfully long time.

That's doesn't sound like good news.

For me, personally, it's not a catastrophic prospect as I can console myself with the thought that I'm going to breathe my last whether the avalanche reaches me or not. But what surprises me is this definite turn society has taken towards pragmatism. People have no time for joy. They are swayed by things that appear paramount right now and can no longer enjoy themselves. They can have fun in the sense that culture has turned into entertainment. Not just in this country but in the West in general. Many people believe they are enjoying culture while watching a reality show or something of the kind. It's not my place to tell anyone what kind of entertainment they should seek. Let everyone find the kind of entertainment they enjoy. But it seems to me that by losing interest in the arts and culture people are depriving themselves of something. I can't understand why someone would renounce this voluntarily. For me it's an opportunity to enjoy life. But maybe the reason they are not interested is that they never even got a whiff of culture and the arts, and don't realise that this kind of joy exists.

What impact does this have?

I really like what Jung once said about art being the most sensitive instrument for recording the soul of a nation. When we lose interest in art we also lose our soul because that's something that needs cultivating.

You have divided your book Fleeting Snow *into sections marked by numbers and letters of the alphabet. Why did you do that?*

It was meant as a helpful gesture towards the reader. If they find a certain plotline or theme boring, they don't have to read on, and can use these markings to skip those passages. And I also thought that it could work like a number of musical motives that flow together towards a finale in a thundering symphony [laughs].

The Kováč character studies language, digging up words nobody knows anymore. How are we affected by the language we speak?

We depend on language and we have to cultivate it. I am afraid that language is becoming increasingly terse. It becomes simplified because we often communicate by means of text messages and emails. And as a result, the only thing that is appreciated in a piece of information is how fast we can get to it. Literature is also a kind of information, but a different kind, it lurks behind laconic sentences or mere words. It seems to me that once you stop using certain words, the things these words denote also begin to die out. If we lack the words necessary to express an experience, we will soon lose the experience itself. George Orwell said that slovenly language makes it easier for us to have foolish thoughts, and if thought corrupts language, language can also corrupt thought. If we allow our language to coarsen or become too simplified, we will also let our thoughts coarsen and simplify. Thought independently of language is not possible.

THE AUTHOR

Pavel Vilikovský (b. 1941) is one of the most important writers of post-Communist Central Europe. He studied film directing in Prague and, later, English and Slovak at Bratislava's Comenius University. One of Slovakia's most distinctive narrative voices, he published only two books under communism – *Citová výchova v marci* / *Sentimental Education in March* (1965) and *Prvá veta spánku* / *The First Sentence of Sleep* (1983), preferring self-imposed silence to self-censorship and working for many years as a literary editor and translator from English. However, since 1989 he has published over a dozen books, notably *Večne je zelený...* (1989; English trans. Charles Sabatos, *Ever Green Is...*, Northwestern University Press, 2002). In 1997 Vilikovský won the *Vilenica Award for Central European Literature*, and he has been twice awarded Slovakia's leading literary prize, the *Anasoft Litera*: in 2006 for the *Magic Parrot and Other Kitschy Stories* and in 2014 for *The First and Last Love*.

THE TRANSLATORS

Julia and **Peter Sherwood** are based in London and work as freelance translators from and into a number of Central and East European languages. Julia Sherwood was born and grew up in Bratislava, Slovakia, and spent more than twenty years in the NGO sector in London before turning to freelance translation some ten years ago. She is *Asymptote's* editor-at-large for Slovakia. Peter Sherwood has had a distinguished academic career at the University of London (School of Slavonic & East European Studies) and the University of North Carolina at Chapel Hill, USA. He published his first translations from the Hungarian over fifty years ago and has since translated works by Béla Hamvas, Noémi Szécsi, Antal Szerb, and Miklós Vámos. Julia and Peter Sherwood's joint book-length translations into English include works by Balla, Daniela Kapitáňová, Uršuľa Kovalyk, Peter Krištúfek (from the Slovak), Hubert Klimko-Dobrzaniecki (Polish), and Petra Procházková (Czech).

First published in 2018 by
Istros Books
London, United Kingdom www.istrosbooks.com

This book was first published in Slovakia as *Letmý sneh*, SLOVART 2014

Cover design and typesetting: Davor Pukljak, www.frontispis.hr

ISBN: 978-1-908236-37-1

Printed by Pulsioprint, France/Bulgaria

This book was published with a financial support from
SLOLIA, Centre for Information on Literature in Bratislava.